MATCH POINT IN CRUMBLETON

CRUMBLETON BOOK 3

BETH RAIN

Copyright © 2024 by Beth Rain

Match Point in Crumbleton (Crumbleton: Book 3)

First Publication: 16th August, 2024

All rights reserved.

No part of this book may be reproduced in any form or by any electronic or mechanical means, including information storage and retrieval systems. Except for use in any review, the reproduction or utilization of this work, in whole or in part, in any form by any electronic, mechanical or other means now known or hereafter invented, is forbidden without the written permission of the publisher.

Published by Beth Rain. The author may be contacted by email on bethrainauthor@gmail.com

❦ Created with Vellum

PROLOGUE

CRUMBLETON TIMES AND ECHO - 22ND AUGUST

What's on This Week

Curating Crumbleton – One Artefact at a Time!

A warm welcome this week to Crumbleton Museum's brand new curator. Cath Walker will be taking on the mammoth task of cataloguing and curating the vast collection at the town museum. The poor old place has been left to its own devices for far too long – so this is likely to be quite a week for our new resident! I'm sure the whole town will rally around – show your support to Cath while she dives in and uses her expertise to get the doors open again. Who knows what amazing treasures lurk inside…

BETH RAIN

Cobbling It All Together

Andy Morgan will be working on the high street cobbles again this week. He'd like to respectfully request that everyone takes the hill at a sensible speed - if you have to drive up it at all. Parts will be cordoned off, making it very narrow in places. Andy will do his best to minimise disruption – although it would be greatly appreciated if parents could encourage their youngsters *not* to use the back of his head as target practise after they've visited the sweetshop. I've been told by a reliable source that a Cola Cube to the back of the head hurts!

Caroline Cook. Editor

CHAPTER 1

CATH

'That's it then love, we're off!'

Cath raised her eyebrows and glared at Bruce. The older of the two removal guys didn't even flinch as he slammed the back doors of the dented white van closed and dusted his hands together.

There was something worryingly final about the action.

'What do you mean, *that's it?!*' said Cath.

Her voice sounded weary, even to her own ears. She was tired—bone tired—and not just because it was moving day at long last. This feeling had been building inside her ever since her husband of fifteen years had announced that he was bored. Bored with their home. Bored with their life together. Most of all, bored with her.

That moment had triggered an exhausting chain of

events that had included hunting for a new job, a new home... and a new life.

Now here she was, standing on Crumbleton's cobbled high street, surrounded by dozens of boxes and the few pitiful bits of furniture she'd brought with her.

What amounted to all her worldly goods were currently blocking the narrow pavement plus a good portion of the frontage of Crumbleton Bookshop. It was long past closing time, and their lights were out... which was probably just as well. It was going to take ages to ferry everything up the narrow staircase to her new flat!

'We need to get a shift on,' said Bruce. 'Can't stay here blocking the high street.'

'Oh,' said Cath, her tone suddenly more hopeful, 'you just mean you need to move the van? That's fair enough. Then we can make a start on getting this lot upstairs. It shouldn't take too long with the three of us.'

'Nope, we're *off* off,' said Bruce, shaking his head. 'We're done. Finished. The end. Finito. I want to get back up to London this evening.'

The young lad who'd helped turf her boxes out of the van nodded from his perch on the passenger seat. He'd already pulled his seatbelt back on and was busy fiddling with his mobile phone.

'But... surely you're going to help me carry everything upstairs first?' she said, glancing at the mountain of boxes again. Okay, perhaps *mountain* was over-egging the pudding a bit. It was more like a *molehill* of boxes considering that it represented her entire life. Still—mountain or molehill—she really *could* do with a hand.

'Gotta go!' said Bruce, shaking his head again.

'But I paid you!' said Cath.

She cringed at the distinct wobble that had just crept into her voice. She wasn't sure if she wanted to burst into tears, yell, or laugh at the ridiculousness of the situation. Frankly, all three options sounded like they'd take way more energy than she had left to spare, so she bit her lip instead.

'You paid us to transport the boxes,' said Bruce, executing what she'd come to recognise as his trademark shrug. 'We've done that. I mean, if we're splitting hairs, I should really charge you extra for helping to unload.'

Cath felt herself deflate and the wobble of emotion promptly turned into the flat feeling of defeat. All she wanted to do was curl up on a comfy sofa and go to sleep—preferably under a fluffy blanket. In fact, if she was going to take the fantasy all the way... she wouldn't mind waking up to a gooey slice of chocolate cake, a cup of perfectly made Earl Grey in her favourite cup, and a half-naked demi-god busily unpacking all her boxes and arranging her new flat for her.

'Fat chance,' she muttered, sinking down to sit on the worn stone doorstep between the bakery and the bookshop.

She watched as Bruce climbed up into the van. Two seconds later, he drove off without so much as a *fare-thee-well.*

'Well,' she sighed, 'this pretty much sucks!'

It definitely wasn't how she'd imagined beginning this new chapter of her life. She'd been hoping for a certain sense of triumph as she started over with her new flat, new job and—with any luck—new friends. Instead, here she was, all alone and feeling a bit... stranded.

Closing her eyes, Cath sucked in a deep breath and was instantly comforted by the faint aroma of fresh cake and homemade bread wafting towards her from the bakery next door. The sign on their door might say *closed*, but that lingering scent felt like a warm welcome to the little town she was going to have to learn to call "home".

'Tomorrow, I'll get a fresh loaf and some cake,' she promised herself quietly, hauling herself back to her feet.

This was the one drawback of rocking up after closing time—she couldn't even grab a sugary treat to give herself a bit of a boost. It had been her new landlord's suggestion to wait until after everyone had gone home for the day before braving the high street with the removals van.

Cath hadn't met Oli in person yet, but she'd been grateful for his email full of meter readings and details about the flat above the bookshop that she'd just rented from him. He'd included a few suggestions about how to make her moving day as easy as possible, too.

Cath might not be able to lay her hands on an emergency piece of chocolate cake right now, but other than that, Oli's advice had been spot-on. Thanks to him, Bruce hadn't had to deal with any other traffic on the narrow, winding hill, and she'd known to leave her car outside town in the Marsh Carpark and walk up. Even better, with all the shops shut for the day, the gaggles of tourists had gone home—so at least her vast heap of stuff on the pavement was less likely to cause a pile-up!

Of course, it *was* a bit of a shame that she couldn't pop into the bookshop to introduce herself to Oli in person. Not that she really needed to—she already had the keys to the flat. Ruth from Crumbleton Council had posted them to her along with the huge, ornate key for the museum and the Welcome Pack for her new job as the curator. She'd included a note of apology that she wouldn't be around for Cath's first few weeks because she was off on holiday to Greece.

Cath didn't mind that much. She rather relished the idea of having free rein with the museum while she found her way around and made some plans for the place. She'd discovered a list of phone numbers in the Welcome Pack, with instructions to "call any of them" if she had any problems. The thought of bothering random strangers made Cath more than a little bit nervous, and she'd instantly vowed only to use them as a last resort. After all, she hadn't actually met any of the locals in person yet - the entire interview process had taken place online.

With any luck, her first few weeks would be plain sailing. What could go wrong at a museum?! That said, what would she know?! Cath hadn't even set foot inside the place yet—there could be all manner of problems waiting to greet her.

There had been several times over the past few weeks when Cath had felt like her impending move to Crumbleton was a dream she might wake up from at any moment.

'As long as it doesn't turn out to be a nightmare,' she sighed.

Ruth had made a few comments during the interview that made Cath suspect she was going to have her work cut out for her. Still… there was nothing like a bit of hard work to help you settle into a new place, was there?

A little wriggle of excitement ran through her as she thought about her new job. Cath couldn't wait to explore the museum and put her own stamp on the collections there. Her official start date wasn't for a few days, but she was planning to head up the hill first thing in the morning to take a look around and get a feel for what she'd let herself in for.

Cath wasn't too worried. She wasn't afraid of hard work, and frankly, it would make a nice change from the art gallery she'd been in charge of for the past few years. That place was beyond pretentious—filled with self-important exhibitions and an air of superiority.

Of course, it didn't help that it belonged to her ex-husband.

Cath straightened her shoulders. She wasn't going to think about him right now. He was firmly in the past, and she had her future to sort out. She had boxes to move, and a new life to settle into. Plus, she really needed that cuppa... she just needed to locate the kettle first!

The thought made her let out a low groan. There was no telling which of these boxes she'd stashed it in. She really should have been a bit more careful when she'd been labelling them. Ah well... perhaps if she started the hunt for it now, there might be some chance of tea before midnight!

Grabbing the nearest box labelled "Kitchen", Cath headed through the front door and took the unfamiliar staircase slowly. Leaving all her belongings unattended outside while she carried the boxes upstairs one by one was hardly ideal. But this wasn't the city... it would be okay, wouldn't it? She'd just have to work as fast as she could to get everything stashed away safely upstairs.

Cursing Bruce under her breath, Cath struggled to open the door at the top of the stairs without dropping her heavy load. Pushing it open with her foot, she glanced around the unfamiliar space. She hadn't had much chance to get a good feel for it yet, but considering she'd agreed to rent it without actually seeing it first, she had to admit that it looked like she'd landed on her feet.

The flat was small, but it felt cosy rather than cramped. The kitchen and living room were open plan, divided by a counter flanked by a couple of high stools. The sitting area was lovely and light, even at this time of the evening, thanks to two huge skylights offering views of the clouds as they skimmed across the sky.

Thankfully, Oli had included some of his larger bits of furniture in the rental agreement. Cath had practically taken his arm off at the offer of all the basics, plus a three-seater sofa. She'd figured that she could always spruce it up with a colourful throw if she didn't like it. Looking at it now, though, she knew there was no way she'd be covering this beauty up. In fact, it was as much as she could do not to slump straight down into its patchwork depths for a snooze. But no... but there were boxes to move before she could even think of putting her feet up!

'On that note...!' she muttered, plonking the first box down onto the kitchen island and darting for the door.

Cath edged sideways through the living room, squeezing between the teetering stacks of boxes as she searched for a spot to place the narrow bookshelf she was carrying. She was exhausted, out of breath, and starting to feel the effects of running up and down the stairs for over an hour with no respite.

Leaning the shelves carefully up against the living room wall, Cath let out a long breath and stared around. The little flat had morphed from cosy to seriously cramped now that she'd brought up the majority of her stuff. The idea that she still had to unpack and sort through it all was more than a little bit daunting. Still, at least this part of the job was nearly done. There was just a giant bag of clothes and a couple of the heavier bits of furniture left down on the pavement. She'd soon be able to have a bit of a breather before phase two commenced.

'Knock knock?!'

A tap on the door followed by an unfamiliar voice made Cath jump.

'Hello?' she squeaked, turning awkwardly on the spot and peering over a stack of boxes. There were two people grinning at her. The man was holding her chunky coffee table as though it weighed no more than a feather. The woman next to him had the handles of Cath's huge tartan laundry bag clutched in her hands, and a packed shopping bag slung over her shoulder.

'Cath?' said the man. 'I'm Oli—and this is Ruby, my much better half!'

Rubbing the grubby cuffs of her jumper across her face just in case she looked as sweaty as she felt, Cath plastered on a smile and picked her way towards them.

'It's so good to meet you,' she said, relieving Ruby of the heavy bag. 'Thanks for bringing these up!'

'A pleasure,' said Oli, placing the coffee table down next to the sofa. 'Though it looks like your guys have almost finished the job!'

'My guys?' laughed Cath. 'Fat chance. They cleared off the moment the van was empty. I'm almost done though.'

'You're kidding?' said Ruby, staring around. 'You brought all this up by yourself? You must be knackered! See, I told you we should have come down sooner.' She elbowed Oli in the ribs.

'Oi!' he laughed, swerving to avoid a second jab. 'I just didn't want to crowd you the minute you arrived,' he added, turning to Cath with an apologetic smile. 'Crumbleton can be full-on, but if I'd have known you were doing all this on your own—'

'It's fine,' said Cath, cutting him off with a smile. 'It's lovely to meet you both, though! I'd offer you a cup of tea, but I haven't unearthed the kettle yet.'

'Don't worry about that,' said Oli.

'Yeah—we come bearing gifts!' said Ruby, patting her shopping bag. 'If you don't mind me gate-crashing your new kitchen, I'll have you sorted in a jiffy.'

'Be my guest,' said Cath in weary amusement.

'And I'll bring up the last few bits of your stuff,' said Oli.

'You don't have to...!' said Cath, more than aware that her protest was just for show. Her arms were throbbing, and her legs felt like lead weights. She was running on fumes by this point.

'He definitely *does* have to!' said Ruby. 'We know how knackering it is to move house—and we only moved from here to the top of the hill. We had tons of help getting our stuff up there... and I swear I still needed to sleep for a week afterwards. We still haven't unpacked everything, but at least that place is bigger so there's more room to stash the boxes until we get around to it. This place is...'

'Cosy!' said Cath with a tired smile.

'Yup – that's one way of putting it.'

'Is that why you moved out?' asked Cath curiously, perching on one of the high stools at the kitchen island. She watched as Ruby unpacked her shopping bag, setting out a box of tea bags, a small jar of instant coffee, and several promising-looking white paper bags that looked like they might have come from the bakery.

'Yep,' Ruby nodded. 'This is a lovely home for one person... two at a push. But I'm a writer and I work from home, so we needed a bit more space. I can get a little bit scary when I'm on deadline! Milly offered us her place over the flower shop when she moved onto Murray's boat out in the marshes—and we grabbed it before anyone else could jump in. It's perfect for us. There are more bedrooms, so I've turned one into an office.'

'Perfect timing for me too!' said Cath. 'Sounds like it's pretty hardcore getting your hands on anywhere to rent in the centre of Crumbleton. I swear I thought I was going to have to turn the job down at one point if I couldn't find anywhere.'

'It can be practically impossible,' laughed Ruby. 'But Caroline mentioned to Ruth that Oli was going to rent out this flat, and she grabbed it for you before Oli even had the chance to advertise it.'

'Lucky for me,' said Cath, reeling slightly at the mention of yet another new name. She wondered if she'd ever figure out who they all were – Milly, Murray, Caroline…

'Now,' said Ruby, giving her a shrewd look. 'I'm betting you haven't even had a drink since you arrived?'

Cath shook her head. 'My kettle is… in one of these boxes. Somewhere. Maybe!'

'Lucky I stashed this in here earlier, then,' said Ruby, bending down to retrieve an electric kettle from the cupboard under the sink. 'And there's milk in the fridge, plus eggs, cheese, butter… and I've got a fresh loaf and some pastries here.'

'Are you serious?' said Cath.

'Dead serious,' said Ruby. 'Welcome to Crumbleton.'

CHAPTER 2

ANDY

*A*ndy came to a halt outside the bakery. Turning to face back down the hill, he took a deep breath that morphed into a yawn halfway through. Staring out across the marshes beyond Crumbleton, a broad smile appeared on his face. It was his favourite time of day.

The sun was just coming up and the little town was quiet in a way that never happened at any other time of day. The tourists were all still in bed, worn out from an overdose of sunshine and sweets the day before. Geraldine, who owned the antique shop at the top of town, would have finished her midnight delivery and re-stocking mission by now, so he'd be safe from her battered van trundling up and down the high street.

With any luck, Andy would have a couple of hours to work on this stretch of cobbles without being bothered by vehicles *or* flying cola cubes. He had no idea why the back of his head had recently become the target of choice for the local youngsters—maybe it was just karma from when he and his mates used to plague old Geordie Jones when they were kids! Perhaps it just came with the job. Still, it certainly made him grateful for his hard hat!

Sucking in another deep breath of fresh morning air, Andy stretched his neck this way and that, still admiring the sky over the marshes as the sun-streaked it with buttercup-gold. It was going to be a good day. He loved being outdoors—and there was nothing better than working in the ancient town where he'd lived all his life.

Andy knew this made him appear unadventurous to some people. He'd been accused of having no ambition... but was that such a bad thing, when he was already living a life he loved?

Some people certainly thought so!

Andy shrugged. Frankly, *some people* could go take a running jump. He knew how lucky he was. After all, how many people could genuinely say they were happy every single day? He was who he was, and he wasn't about to apologise for enjoying the simple things life had to offer.

Speaking of simple things... today was going to be an *extra-special* kind of good day. He was going to be working right outside the bakery for the next few hours, and the scent coming from the ovens inside was already making his stomach growl. Hot sugar, cinnamon, allspice and fruit mixed with fresh bread.

Heaven on earth!

Of course, it *did* help that his sister owned the bakery. Heather was almost guaranteed to bring him something fresh from the oven for a second breakfast a little bit later on. With any luck, it would be one of her fruit slices. They were Andy's favourites—rich and delicious and drizzled with icing. She only made them on certain days… but as luck would have it, today was one of them.

It was going to be the perfect day—he could feel it in his bones!

Just the thought of the impending sweet treat had his mouth watering… but first, he needed to get on with the job he'd come to do.

With one last glance out across the marshes, Andy turned to the wheelbarrow he always had with him when he was working. It was the perfect way to cart around all the basic tools he needed to do his job—levelling up and repairing the town's acres of ancient cobblestones.

The old barrow might not look like much, but it was far less of a nuisance than trying to find somewhere to park a van on the high street while he worked.

Grabbing his stack of orange traffic cones, Andy swiftly set them out around the patch of pavement right outside the bakery window. The stones had become loose and raised, and were "a lawsuit waiting to happen," according to the town council. They were always grumbling about the impracticality of the old cobbles, but Andy loved them—and not just because they meant he had a steady supply of work. To him, they were something ancient and beautiful that simply needed a bit of care and attention to help them last another several hundred years.

'Hey, little brother! Come to hang out with me today, have you?'

Andy glanced up from his crouched position, only to find Heather beaming down at him as she wiped flour from her hands with a checked tea towel.

'Yep—gotta sort out this little lot,' he said, nodding at the patch of raised stones. 'And FYI, I've got plenty of greys in this lot now,' he added, lifting his hard hat and running his hand over his thick mop of hair. 'I'm not sure you can call me *little brother* anymore!'

'Give over, you'll always be my annoying little brother,' said Heather with a wink. 'Anyway, do you reckon you'll be finished by the time I open?'

'I'll do my best,' said Andy.

'No rush,' said Heather with a shrug. 'I was just gauging when to bring you a fruit slice.'

'Any time is a good time for a fruit slice,' said Andy. He might have had breakfast less than half an hour ago, but his stomach growled in anticipation of the promised treat.

'I'll be as quick as I can,' said Heather. 'We've got to

MATCH POINT IN CRUMBLETON

keep you well fuelled, considering you single-handedly keep this town in one piece.'

'Oh, I don't know about that,' chuckled Andy.

'Let's face it, there probably isn't a single part of Crumbleton you *haven't* had to repair over the years!' said Heather.

'Well, some things deserve a bit of TLC,' he said, giving the cobbles a friendly pat. 'I mean, even with the limited traffic allowed up here, these poor old things get a serious battering. Did you know some of them date as far back as the thirteen hundreds? The ones up by the museum are—'

Andy broke off and rolled his eyes at Heather, who was busily executing an exaggerated yawn.

'Oi!' he laughed. 'Some people have no soul.'

'Not when there's bread to be baked and fruit slices to ice and you want to give me a history lesson about cobblestones... again!'

'Fine, you win!' said Andy. 'I'm just saying, it'd be a real shame if the council got their way and tarmacked over the whole lot.'

'They wouldn't?!' gasped Heather.

'They've definitely talked about it,' said Andy. 'The subject usually comes up whenever the utility companies leave a mess behind them and the town has to pay me extra to put it right.'

'But... you're way cheaper than pouring tarmac down the entire hill!' said Heather, looking horrified.

'I am,' said Andy with a nod. 'Besides, I think the

tourist draw of our pretty cobblestones will always win them over. At least, that's what I keep telling myself.'

'Yeah, that and the fact that Crumbleton is so steep, the tarmac would probably ooze down into a great big puddle near the City Gates,' laughed Heather. 'I'm sure it'd make a horrible mess of the oldest ones up by the museum first, though!'

'Mean!' gasped Andy.

Heather grinned at him.

'Speaking of the museum, have you met the new person yet?' he said. 'The who's taken on the curation job? I thought she was meant to be arriving soon.'

'She's already here,' said Heather.

Andy frowned. 'Why exactly did you point at the sky when you said that?'

'Because,' said Heather, 'she moved into Oli's flat last night.'

'Then we've probably just woken the poor woman up!' said Andy, dropping his voice to a stage whisper.

'Nah,' said Heather.

'How'd you know that?' he said in surprise.

'Because I saw her leave the flat and wander off up the hill about five minutes before you appeared.'

'This morning?' said Andy, raising his eyebrows as he glanced down at his battered old watch. 'As in… before six in the morning?'

'Uh huh,' said Heather, looking unperturbed.

'You do realise that's not normal behaviour?' said Andy. 'I mean… for anyone other than us two!'

'Andy love, if you think it's normal to get up this early just to fix twelfth-century cobbles...'

'Actually, this little patch is probably a replacement that happened somewhere around the late seventeen hundreds,' said Andy.

'*Definitely* not normal!' chuckled Heather, shaking her head. 'And anyway, maybe our new curator is just keen.'

'Let's see how long that lasts when she gets to the museum and sees the state of the place,' said Andy, pulling a face. 'I heard that she took the job without even coming down for a look around.'

'Ouch!' said Heather.

'Yeah,' sighed Andy.

He had a feeling the new arrival was in for a bit of a shock—unless Ruth from the council had been scrupulously honest with her... which he somehow doubted.

The castle with its attached museum building needed some serious repairs—but it wasn't just what was going on with the outside that might put her off. Inside, the place was piled high with the detritus of decades.

'Well... let's just hope she sticks around,' said Heather. 'Anyway, I'd better head back inside if you want your fruit slice before lunchtime!'

'Erm sis... isn't that your phone?' said Andy.

They both paused and cocked their heads.

'It is!' said Heather. 'Who on earth's calling at this

time of day?'

Andy shrugged, but the question had obviously been rhetorical as Heather had already dashed inside to answer it.

Grabbing his bucket of sand from the wheelbarrow, Andy started to set out his tools so that he wouldn't have to keep clambering to his feet every five minutes. He was just about to get stuck in when Heather reappeared with the phone clutched in her hand.

'What's up?' he said in surprise.

'It's for you,' said Heather.

CHAPTER 3

CATH

Well, she had to admit it—her new commute beat her old one hands down. Cath clutched her half-drunk mug of Earl Grey as she ambled up the high street, taking deep breaths of the fresh, early-morning air.

And boy, was it early, even for her!

Cath was used to hopping out of bed the moment she woke up—mainly because her old, terraced house had been on one side of the capital and the imposing white cube of the gallery had been on the other. Early mornings had been a necessary evil if she wanted to get to work on time.

Here, though? Well, she had a feeling they might become a bit of a joy instead, especially if the colours dancing at the edges of the wispy clouds were always this enchanting!

Of course, it helped that her commute was now less

than a five-minute walk up the picturesque cobbles to the top of the hill.

Plus, it didn't hurt that the moment she'd closed her new front door behind her, she'd been greeted by the tantalising scent of hot bread. Crumbleton's baker was clearly already hard at work!

Cath hadn't forgotten her promise to herself the previous evening. She had every intention of wandering back down the hill to grab herself a mid-morning treat. But first—she wanted to see what she'd let herself in for at the museum.

Patting her pocket, Cath double-checked that she'd remembered to pick up the ornate key that would let her into her new lair. There wasn't really any need—it was so heavy, she could feel it weighing the side of her cardigan down, bouncing slightly with every step she took. Still, it was nice to hear the reassuring jangle as it rattled against its big, metal ring and the bunch of smaller, unlabelled keys that had come with it. Whether she'd ever figure out what they were all for was anyone's guess!

Cath sighed and smiled as she took another sip of tea. Realistically, she should be exhausted after all the stress and heavy lifting of the day before. That couldn't be further from the truth, though. It might be early, but she was buzzing with possibility. Sure, her new home might look like a badly played game of Jenga right now, but that didn't matter. Give it a few days and she'd get those boxes under control.

Pausing to peer at a gorgeous display of potted orchids and spiny cactuses in the florist's window, Cath peeped up at the sign.

Milly's Flowers

So, this must be where Oli and Ruby had moved to. They hadn't been exaggerating when they'd said they'd been able to transport most of their belongings by hand!

The pair of them had been so kind to her the previous evening. They'd made sure she had everything she needed, and Ruby had even insisted on helping her to make up her bed so that it was ready for her to collapse into the minute she was ready. They'd disappeared fairly promptly—clearly sensing she was so tired she could barely string a sentence together—but not before they'd promised to catch up with her over drinks down at the Dolphin and Anchor as soon as she'd settled in.

Their easy, uncomplicated welcome had made Cath feel instantly at home, and her fears about starting over again and finding new friends had melted away. Now all she had to do was get her teeth into her new job, and she'd be off to a flying start!

'And there's the museum!' Cath whispered to herself.

The sight up ahead of her was quite imposing... at least at first glance. The museum was part of the higgledy-piggledy castle that crowned the top of Crumbleton's hill. It had a creaky-looking bell tower that was something straight out of a fairytale. There were turrets and arrow slits and an impressive, iron-studded wooden door that looked like it could single-handedly hold off a marauding mob.

Cath knew better than to sink too far into the glamour of the fairytale, though. Ruth had hinted during the interview that it wasn't just the inside of the museum that would benefit from a bit of care and attention. The outside needed quite a bit of work too—work that would take a pretty penny to complete.

Even from this distance, it was easy to spot the telltale signs that the stonework needed some serious TLC. Here and there, tufts of grass stuck out of the walls. There were patches where stones had come loose and fallen to the ground far below. A veritable forest of buddleia bushes had taken root in the resulting gaps. As pretty as the purple flowers were—wafting in the breeze several dozen feet above ground level—Cath knew the roots would be playing havoc with the ancient walls.

'Let's get inside!' she murmured, not wanting to get overwhelmed by all the work that needed doing.

Cath trotted past the little antiques shop that lay between *Milly's Flowers* and the museum, fishing the key out of her pocket as she went.

'Oh!' She came to a sudden halt.

Cath had been so caught up with inspecting the building itself that she'd managed to miss a pile of... stuff... right outside the museum entrance.

A knackered-looking sofa had been left on the cobbled pavement next to the door. Balanced on top of it was a ginormous tasselled lampshade, a brown china chicken, and what looked to be an old wooden tennis racket with loose strings.

'And yet more boxes!' said Cath, the words tumbling out in a desperate sort of chuckle.

There were five of them, piled on top of each other and leaning precariously against the door itself. She had no idea what all this stuff was... nor why it was there... but she was going to have to shift it out of the way if she wanted to get inside.

Cath sidled up to the stack of boxes. She didn't want to waste time moving them out of the way one by one, so she hauled them away from the door and then leaned her full weight against the damp cardboard and pushed until the whole lot started to inch sideways.

'There, that'll do,' she said, holding out her hands as she backed away, just in case of imminent collapse. 'Sorted!' she added triumphantly when the stack sagged ever so slightly but failed to topple over.

Straightening her shoulders and reaching back into her pocket for the key, she slotted it into the lock. This was it—her new domain! It was finally time to take a peep inside.

'Three... two... one...' she whispered, before turning the enormous key. Except... it wouldn't turn. In fact, it wouldn't even budge.

'What?' she groaned, taking the key back out of the

lock and staring at it. It didn't look damaged. Surely Ruth had sent her the right one?! 'Try again...'

With far less pomp and circumstance the second time around, Cath shoved the key back into the lock and tried to turn it. It simply wouldn't cooperate.

'Seriously?!' muttered Cath, barging her shoulder against the door... more to let out her frustration rather than anything else. Sure enough, all she managed to do was bounce off the ancient—decidedly solid—wood.

Okay, it was time for Plan B... whatever that was!

Cath rubbed her shoulder and stared around as though the answer might be staring right back at her. Unfortunately, it was barely six o'clock in the morning, and she was in an unfamiliar town. There was no one else around. Perhaps the only answer was to give up, head home, crawl back into bed and admit defeat.

So much for an early start to the perfect first day!

'Nope!' she said, squaring her shoulders. She wasn't about to be beaten by a faulty lock!

Grabbing the bunch of smaller keys, she started to offer them up one by one. After all, she'd just assumed that the great big one was for the front door!

Two seconds later, she gave up again.

'Okay... okay, let's think,' she said, stepping back.

Cath had the Welcome Pack in her bag, but she'd already read the thing from cover to cover more than once, and as far as she could remember, there wasn't any mention of how to actually get inside the place.

But… there *was* that list of emergency phone numbers. She could call someone. At six o'clock in the morning. That was *bound* to help her make friends… *NOT!*

Grabbing the pack from her bag, Cath started leafing through the pages, hunting for the list of numbers. The names hadn't really meant much to her the last time she'd looked, but now as her eyes scanned down the list, she saw that both Ruby and Oli's private mobiles were on there, along with a landline for the bookshop. Well, there was no way she was going to drag those two out of bed this early in the morning—especially after they'd been so kind to her the day before.

Maybe she should just leave it for now? Maybe…

Cath's eyes had come to rest on a number for *Heather*. The name didn't mean anything to her, but it had *Crumbleton Bakery* right next to it. At least she knew she wouldn't be getting Heather out of bed. The lights for the bakery had been on when she'd walked past, and the scent of baking bread was a dead giveaway that there must be someone hard at work in there.

Grabbing her mobile, Cath punched in the number before she could chicken out. She wasn't expecting someone who owned a bakery to help her with a faulty lock… but Heather might at least be able to tell her which of the dozen other names on the list to call.

'Hello? Crumbleton Bakery, this is Heather…'

'Oh, uh, hi!' said Cath, wincing slightly at the nervous squeak in her voice. 'Look, I'm really sorry to bother you... especially so early!'

'Early? Ha!' chuckled the woman on the other end. 'And it's fine, I'm just taking a breather. Now, what can I do for you?'

'I'm Cath... the new curator at the museum. I... erm... I can't get the key to work and...' Cath paused. She sounded utterly ridiculous. She should have just gone home and then tried to reach Ruth when it was a more human hour rather than bugging random strangers. 'Sorry, this is stupid, but I wasn't sure who to call, and I saw your lights on and...'

'Stop!' said Heather. 'And breathe!'

'Okay,' said Cath. 'Breathing!'

'Good!' laughed Heather. 'Now, you need to speak to my brother.'

'Oh!' said Cath in surprise. 'Erm, could I grab his number...? Or maybe he's on my list already. What's his name?'

'No need, I'll go grab him for you now,' said Heather. 'He's working right outside.'

Before Cath could say anything else, there was a load of rustling on the other end of the line, and then she heard muffled voices.

'Hello?' The unfamiliar voice was deep and decidedly gravelly. 'Can't get into the museum? I'll be right up!'

Cath didn't even manage to get a word out before

he hung up on her. Heather's brother was clearly a man of very few words.

Suddenly exhausted by the unexpected turn of events, Cath stared around, looking for somewhere to perch while she waited for her saviour to arrive. She couldn't imagine it would take him very long to wander up the hill from the bakery, but there *was* a perfectly decent sofa right next to her! If she shifted the lampshade over she could just…

'Ahhhh,' she sighed, sinking down into the cushions. That was *seriously* comfortable! Either that or she was just so knackered that even a stone wall would feel like luxury.

Cath had just shifted the china chicken over a bit so that she could pop her bag down next to her when she spotted a tall figure wearing overalls and a hard hat loping towards her up the hill.

Huh! He'd sounded a lot older on the phone.

Cath raised a hand to push her hair away from her face, suddenly wishing that she'd taken the time to put on some mascara before leaving the flat. Scooting forwards, she hauled herself back out of the depths of the sofa to greet him.

CHAPTER 4

ANDY

*A*ndy watched with some amusement as the slender figure that was being eaten by the old sofa in front of the museum struggled to break free. The poor woman wasn't having much luck. The piece of furniture seemed intent on keeping hold of its prey, and she was getting more flustered by the second.

'Hey!' he said, coming to a halt a few feet away from her, just as she managed to regain her feet.

'Hi,' she said, flipping long strands of hair back out of her face as she pinned him with a smile.

Wow.

Okay, so it was safe to say that Andy hadn't been expecting to have the air knocked out of him by a beautiful stranger before he'd had his morning iced fruit slice!

Andy glanced away quickly as she did her best to

yank her cardigan into place and hoik her slim jeans back up where they belonged.

'So... erm... have you tried wiggling it?' he said.

'I *beg* your pardon?' said the woman.

'The key!' gasped Andy. 'I meant the key!'

'Oh, erm... right, of course,' she said. 'No, I didn't. But seriously, it's not going to make any difference. It's really stuck... it won't turn at all and... well, I'm not even sure if this is the right key and—'

'It's the right key,' said Andy gently, cutting across her flustered explanations. 'Give it a go.'

He wasn't sure why she'd just turned such a sweet shade of pink. After all, he was the one busy making a total prat out of himself. The woman shot an indecipherable look at him and he watched as she turned away and slotted the key into the lock.

'Like this?' she said, giving it an exaggerated wiggle. 'Oh!'

Sure enough, the key turned on the first try, and the heavy old door swung open without a sound. Mainly because he'd oiled it the last time he'd taken a bunch of stuff inside.

'It's just old,' said Andy. 'It can get a bit grumpy sometimes.'

'I know the feeling,' muttered the woman, looking even more pink as she turned to face him again. 'I'm *so* sorry to drag you up here on a fool's errand!'

'It's fine,' Andy shrugged. 'I mean, it would have been annoying in about an hour when the fruit slices are ready. I'd hate to be dragged away from the important part of the morning. Oh – I'm Andy by the way.'

'Cath,' said the woman. 'And… fruit slices?'

'My sister's a genius,' said Andy seriously. 'You need to try them. They'll change your life. I know I'm biased because it's Heather… but I swear they're the best thing I've ever tasted.'

'I'll have to pop down to the bakery later then,' said Cath.

'Before they're all gone,' said Andy seriously.

'Well… I think I'd better deal with things here first,' sighed Cath. 'What on earth is all this stuff anyway?' she added, pointing at the boxes and the settee.

'Historical artefacts,' said Andy with a shrug. 'The museum's full of things like this.'

'It is?' said Cath, looking horrified.

'Sure,' Andy nodded. 'People like to have a good turf out… and they don't want to throw away anything with historical significance, so they bring them here instead.'

'Seriously?' said Cath.

Andy could swear that the pink blush had just paled by several degrees.

'Yeah,' he said. 'It's one of the reasons the council have had such a hard time finding someone to take over running the place. It's full of junk and it's falling down. They've only really got the funding to cover your position… so the repairs just get shunted further and further down the list. But... you know all this, right? They showed you around on your interview?'

Cath shook her head.

'They didn't?' said Andy, suddenly feeling like he wanted to reel all his words back into his mouth and swallow them.

'This is the first time I've been up here,' said Cath.

'Since you moved in?' said Andy.

'No. Ever,' said Cath. 'They did my interview online.'

'But... Ruth did a video or something?' said Andy.

He remembered hearing something about it. There had been some chatter about it down at the Dolphin and Anchor and rather a lot of giggling about "convenient camera angles."

'Mmm,' said Cath. 'I could never get that link to work for some reason.'

'Well... deep breath,' said Andy, forcing his voice to sound as light and cheery as he could. He wasn't going to take the blame for scaring off the new curator before she'd even seen inside the museum! 'How about I help you move the sofa and get the rest of this stuff inside while I'm here?'

'Really?' said Cath. 'You don't mind?'

'Of course not,' said Andy. 'I'm not going to abandon you just because you've got the door open.'

'Well... thanks. That'd be great,' said Cath.

The beaming smile she shot in his direction promptly made Andy feel like he'd been thumped in the chest again. Out of instinct, he raised his hand to run his fingers through his hair—only to discover he was still wearing his hard hat.

What a prat!

He quickly grabbed the peak of the less-than-flattering item of headgear and yanked it off, ruffling his hair to get rid of the flat ring he knew would be there.

What was this woman doing to him? One smile from her and he seemed to be morphing into an image-conscious teenager, keen to impress the girl. Well... he wasn't off to the best of starts, was he? So far, he'd managed to tell her to wiggle, and then frightened her half to death about her new job.

Smooth, Andy! Seriously smooth.

His only excuse was that he was thoroughly out of practice around beautiful women. Or... any women, really. He hadn't dated anyone for months. Actually, make that years.

But what was he thinking about dating for?! Cath was probably married, for heaven's sake. And no, he *wouldn't* glance at her ring finger to check.

'You... erm... you coming?' said Cath, snapping Andy back to reality.

'Er... sure,' he said. 'Shall we start with the sofa?'

'I was thinking... shall we start by turning the lights on inside?' said Cath.

'Good plan!' laughed Andy. 'Sure you're up for this?'

'Not sure I've got much choice in the matter now,' said Cath with a shrug. 'I've signed the contract.'

Andy nodded and led the way.

'The bank of light switches are just around here to the right,' he said, moving slowly along the hallway and hoping he didn't trip over any concealed "artefacts". 'Here we go,' he added, coming to a halt in front of the gloomy patch of wall. Reaching up, he went to flick on the first row of switches, only for his hand to press down on top of Cath's fingers.

'Oh, sorry!' she gasped.

'My fault!' muttered Andy. 'You go ahead. It's the top two rows you want, and then the middle two switches on the fourth.'

'Okay... I... okay...' said Cath.

'I'll run outside and start bringing in the boxes,' he muttered, practically jogging away from her before he could do anything else to embarrass himself.

CHAPTER 5

CATH

Finding space for the sofa and random junk from outside hadn't been as easy as it sounded. Thank goodness for Andy's help. Cath wasn't entirely convinced that she'd have managed it on her own. Together, they'd shifted a few things around inside so there was just enough floor space for the new additions.

Now that Andy had left her to it—with a promise to buy her a "welcome to Crumbleton" fruit slice when she needed a break—Cath finally had the chance to take a breath and have a proper look around. Up until that point, she'd simply been too distracted. Andy's presence had been... all-consuming.

'Don't be an idiot,' she muttered, turning on the spot as she surveyed the chaos around her.

Idiot or not, she knew what her hot cheeks meant. She'd basically been blushing continuously from the moment Andy had said his first "hey". When his hand had landed on top of hers as they'd both reached for the light switches... well, put it like this, she'd be contacting an electrician to check those things were safe. There simply had to be a fault, because there was no way a bit of fleeting contact with Andy's warm, rough fingers could have caused *that* many sparks.

Besides, Cath wasn't interested. Not in men, or dating, or men... or dating. Or any kind of romantic relationship. At all. Possibly ever again.

It doesn't have to be romantic though, does it? It could just be physical!

'Shut up shut up shut up!' she muttered at her inner floozie, pushing her hair back off her burning face. 'Focus!'

Cath thrust all thoughts of Andy firmly to the back of her mind. She had a sneaking suspicion they wouldn't stay put for long, but right now, she had a job to do.

Picking her way through the jumble of boxes in front of her, Cath started to survey the scene properly for the first time. In a way, she was glad she'd accepted the job without having a look around first because this was... a lot. So much so, that anyone volunteering to take it on after seeing it would have to have some kind of screw loose. The sheer scale of what she was going to have to contend with was overwhelming.

It wasn't just the mess of boxes and donations that

was the problem either. It was the fact that there didn't seem to be any kind of logic to the museum. At all.

Cath was pretty sure there were display cases in there somewhere, hidden deep behind teetering piles of unidentified *stuff*—but other than the occasional tell-tale gleam of glass here and there, they were practically invisible from where she was standing.

Wondering if she should leave a trail of breadcrumbs so that she'd be able to find her way back out, Cath started to edge her way deeper into the room. It took some doing, and it wasn't long before she had to tie her cardigan around her waist.

'Ah ha! An actual display!' she cheered as she rounded a tower of junk only to spot the side of a glass case in front of her.

Weirdly, it looked like it held a collection of sports memorabilia. There was a wooden tennis racket similar to the one that had been waiting for her on the sofa outside, and a couple of old, motheaten balls. What tennis had to do with Crumbleton's history was anyone's guess... but it *looked* like the collection had been put together on purpose. Then again, it could just be a bunch of random tat that had been thrown into a cabinet to get it out of the way.

Clambering over a couple of boxes so that she could take a closer look, Cath cupped her hands against the dusty glass and peered inside. She could only see the top couple of shelves. There was a pair of grubby shorts pinned to a disintegrating backboard, along with a couple of very unsavoury-looking sweatbands.

Cath wrinkled her nose and stepped back again. For some reason, she'd been expecting to find a lot more maritime memorabilia and old fishing gear, what with Crumbleton's coastal connections. There was definitely a net in the case... but it wasn't the kind she'd been anticipating... and it looked like it would take about a decade to get it untangled.

'Where am I meant to start?' said Cath, turning away from the tatty tennis gear and nearly breaking her neck on an ancient-looking piece of machinery that had splatters of white paint all over it. 'Sorry, old thing!' she muttered, giving one of the handles an apologetic pat. She might not know what it was, but it was the first thing she'd seen in here that actually looked like it belonged in a museum!

Picking her way back through the maze, Cath started to look more closely at the state of things. It was a real mess, but at least there didn't seem to be any signs of water damage or things being chewed by mice... or worse.

Cath shuddered and pulled a face at the thought. In a weird way, it was a bit of a shame. Even though she didn't fancy having to deal with a bunch of furry, chew-happy squatters, they might have made things a bit simpler. There was no doubt in her mind that she was going to have to thin down this collection quite a bit... and a spot of water damage or some thorough chewing might have given her the perfect starting place to start binning a few things.

No such luck!

Now and again, Cath stopped to shift a box or inspect a piece of random furniture so that she could see what was behind or inside. All she found was yet more boxes! Her grand plans of throwing the doors open to visitors again by the end of the following week were fading fast... just like her levels of energy and enthusiasm.

'Andy was right,' she muttered, as she finally reached the front of the building again, 'I need a sugary treat!'

A cup of tea was definitely in order, and if she could wangle a fruit slice out of the bakery before they'd even opened, all the better. With any luck, Andy would be a man of his word and wheedle one for her as well as himself!

Grabbing her handbag from where she'd stashed it in a dusty corner near the door, Cath flicked the lights back off—noting the distinct lack of sparks this time—and beat a retreat, yanking the door closed behind her.

For a second, she was half-tempted to leave the museum unlocked... just in case there were any friendly burglars around who might do her the favour of nicking some of the not-so-priceless artefacts.

'Better not,' she said with a grin, sliding the key into the lock and turning it. Nothing happened. 'Are you serious?!'

Taking a deep breath, Cath remembered Andy's instructions and proceeded to give the key an elaborate wiggle as she tried again. It turned smoothly. It was clearly easy, once you knew how!

Pocketing the key, Cath paused for a brief moment. It was hard not to feel like she was running away. She'd had a feeling the place was going to be in a bit of a state, but she hadn't really been expecting this peculiar combination of town-jumble-sale, giant recycling bin, and abandoned storage unit.

'I need cake,' she muttered, setting off before she could guilt herself into going back inside.

The wooden shutters were still pulled across the antiques shop window as Cath marched past. It was no great surprise considering it probably hadn't even reached eight o'clock in the morning yet. The sign taped to the door read "Open at 10.30(ish)"

The *ish* part made her smile. Anyone who put that on their opening hours *had* to be a bit of a character, didn't they? She could only imagine she'd get to know her new work neighbour before too long. In fact, she'd make sure she did. Having a museum and an antiques shop right next door to each other had to offer some kind of opportunity to work together, didn't it?!

As she wandered towards the bakery, Cath realised her stomach was tight with nervous knots. Somehow, she didn't think it was entirely down to the fact that she'd just left the biggest mess she'd ever witnessed behind her at the top of the hill. She had a feeling it had something to do with... Andy?

No, that would be ridiculous!

Cath gave herself a little shake. Sure, he seemed nice—if a bit quiet. He definitely wasn't too hard on the eyes, either, especially when he took off his hard hat. Even so—she'd promised herself to stay away from all men for the foreseeable future.

Greg had broken something inside her when he'd pulled the rug of her life out from beneath her feet. Cath wasn't entirely sure if the damage was in her head or in her heart. Perhaps it was both. Either way, that wonderful, floaty belief that there might be someone out there to share the rest of her life with had been well and truly shattered.

There would be no romance in her future. It didn't matter. She had plenty of other things to keep her busy. A new flat to turn into a home, for one thing. The museum for another. She definitely had her work cut out for her there! She wouldn't have time for ridiculous things like romance and new relationships.

Squaring her shoulders, Cath forced herself to smile and think of the positives. She'd moved to a lovely new town. She had a new job, and she'd already met some nice people.

'Hey!' she said, her forced smile instantly feeling more natural on her face as she spotted Andy leaning up against the doorway of the bakery. There was a woman with him, laughing as she watched him wave his hard hat in front of his face as though he was halfway through a hot flush.

'Cath!' he spluttered, sounding slightly pained. 'This is Heather… my… ouch… *ha ho heee hooooot!*… my sister!'

'Hi,' said Cath, smiling uncertainly at Heather, who beamed back at her. 'Erm… is he okay?'

'Other than being an impatient idiot, he's fine!' laughed Heather. 'He never waits for his fruit slice to cool down enough before she shoves it in his face!'

'Ooh, that's the problem!' said Cath, spotting a steaming piece of cake in Andy's hand that she hadn't noticed before because of all the hat-flapping.

'Blow on it, idiot!' said Heather. 'Seriously, he didn't even give me a chance to ice it before he demanded a piece.'

'Ha! Hoooo!' hooted Andy, having taken another steaming mouthful, only to suck in air and waft his hat again as though his life depended on it.

'It's your own fault if you've burned your tongue,' huffed Heather.

'Is that the mythical fruit slice I've heard so much about?' said Cath, taking a deep sniff of the sweet, spice-infused air wafting from the bakery.

'Yep,' said Heather. 'I suppose you'll be wanting a piece now?'

Cath grinned at Heather and nodded enthusiastically. 'Yes please!'

'I'll go and grab you a bit,' said Heather. 'Give me a

sec to add some icing... and just learn from this idiot,' she added, nodding at Andy. 'It's stupidly hot!'

'So good though!' said Andy, giving Heather the thumbs up.

'Idiot,' muttered Heather again before disappearing back inside.

'I thought the boxes might beat you before too long,' said Andy, giving her a mischievous look.

'Oh, I'm not beaten that easily,' said Cath drawing herself up. 'Just tempted by the mention of cake.'

'It's definitely tempting!' said Andy, licking his fingers.

Cath shifted her weight, wondering why her knees suddenly felt a bit wobbly. She clearly needed the sugar hit more than she'd realised.

'Anyway—I just thought I'd regroup and make a plan before diving in for the next round,' said Cath.

'Good idea,' said Andy, nodding.

When he didn't say anything else, Cath glanced over her shoulder, hoping that Heather would reappear and save her from the awkward silence. No such luck.

'So... erm... how's your morning going?' she said.

Andy pointed at a patch of cobblestones enclosed within a ring of orange roadwork cones and striped safety tape. They'd clearly been re-laid. She'd almost face-planted over a couple of raised stones the previous day when she'd been unloading the van. Now though, they were back in position and the beautiful pattern of the road surface had been restored.

'Nice work,' she said. She instantly wanted to kick herself. 'Sorry, that sounded like I was taking the piss... but they look brilliant.'

'Cheers,' said Andy with an easy grin. 'I've had a good bit of practice with Crumbleton's cobbles by this point, mind.'

'Oh God,' sighed Heather, reappearing at Cath's side. 'Don't get him talking about the blasted cobbles. He'll personally introduce you to every single one of them and give you a history lesson while he's at it if you don't watch out.'

Andy rolled his eyes at his sister, and Cath grinned at the easy sibling banter.

'Here,' said Heather, thrusting one of two white paper bags towards Cath. 'Remember—seriously hot! I'm not sure how much of the icing will have stayed put.'

'Ooh, thanks!' said Cath, opening the bag and taking a deep sniff. Her stomach instantly let out a growl that was loud enough to shake the bakery windows. Her eyes went wide with mortification, but Heather just laughed.

'Yeah—I think I'm going to like you if that's the way you react to my baking!'

CHAPTER 6

ANDY

*A*ndy couldn't tear his eyes away from Cath as she blew on the hot fruit slice before taking a careful nibble from the edge. He grinned as her eyes lit up with delight.

'Oh. My. Goodness!' she murmured. 'Heather, you're a genius!'

'Isn't she?!' said Andy. 'See, I told you.'

'You, little brother, are a cake pusher!' laughed Heather.

'Yeah, yeah!' said Andy, popping the last piece of his still-steaming cake into his mouth. Why was it that the last bite was always the best?

'I don't mind him getting me hooked on something when it tastes this good!' said Cath, taking another careful bite. She clearly wasn't up for scalding the roof of her mouth like he had.

Heather opened her own bag and took a bite,

leaning back against the wooden doorjamb of the bakery with a contented sigh.

'Okay,' she said, 'not bad, even if I do say so myself!'

'Now try saying that without steam pouring out of your mouth,' chuckled Andy.

'Not possible,' Heather shrugged. 'Anyway, Cath—has the state of the museum managed to scare you off yet?'

Andy frowned as he glanced at Cath, watching for her reaction. For some reason, he was flooded with relief when she shook her head.

'Absolutely not,' she said, and there was a hint of steel to her voice. 'I mean... I like a challenge.'

'Just as well!' said Heather. 'From what Andy said, it sounds like what's-her-name from the council wasn't exactly forthcoming about the state of the place when you had your interview?'

'Well... maybe not,' said Cath. 'I mean, I guess I wasn't expecting quite so much random junk... but I *was* expecting at least a couple of decent displays already in place that I could build on. Never mind. I'll get it sorted. Somehow.'

'Well, you're a braver woman than me,' said Heather. 'I wouldn't even know where to start.'

'Why do you think I'm down here with you guys instead of back up there!' said Cath with a sheepish smile.

'Well, if there's anything we can do...' said Andy.

'Actually, I wanted to ask—what's with all the old

tennis gear?' said Cath. 'Any ideas? I found the remains of some kind of display... and there was that old racket outside too. Crumbleton's on a hill. Is there even a tennis court here?'

Andy nodded, doing his best to surreptitiously brush fruit slice crumbs from the front of his overalls as he did so. 'Yep. At least, there used to be... down at the Dolphin and Anchor. The place didn't start life as a hotel, believe it or not. It used to be the headquarters of the Crumbleton on the Hill Lawn Tennis Club.'

'You're kidding?' said Cath.

'This place always had ideas above its station,' laughed Heather.

'But... where was the court?' said Cath.

'It's around the back,' said Andy. 'You wouldn't know that's what it used to be. It's a slightly overgrown bit of garden now—which is my fault because I need to get down there and put the mower around. They use it for wedding photos now, but there used to be a pristine grass court. Apparently, they served strawberries and cream on a covered terrace after every game.'

'That fell down ages ago,' said Heather.

'Sounds wonderful,' said Cath.

'There was a members bar too, and changing rooms and everything,' said Andy. 'Apparently, it was all very grand.'

'But... it's not there anymore?' said Cath. 'I mean, no one plays tennis down there these days?'

'Nah, not for ages,' said Andy. 'Of course, Heather might remember it. She's a lot more ancient than I am.'

'Oi, you cheeky blighter!' said Heather, leaning forward to poke him in the stomach. 'Less of that cheek or your cake supply's cut off!'

Andy grinned at her.

'Seriously Cath, don't believe a word out of his mouth. I'm three years older than him... and he's a bloomin' spring chicken. For the record, the tennis club has been closed for years. And when I say years, I mean decades!'

'That seems like a shame,' said Cath.

'It was all well and good when they were playing using the old wooden rackets,' said Andy, 'but the minute things started to get a bit more high tech and the balls could be walloped faster and further, there were a lot of complaints from the neighbours about broken windows. It didn't take long for the place to close down after that. Then Fergus bought the building and turned it into what it is today.'

'Must have been about thirty or forty years ago,' said Heather. 'Obviously, the building itself is even older and predates the tennis club. It was built by some crazy dude who liked playing snooker.'

'Crazy in what way?' said Cath, cocking her head at Andy in a way that made him feel strangely breathless. It was only Heather's knowing look that loosened his tongue. He could really do without his sister ribbing him about Cath. The poor woman had only just arrived in town!

'To be fair,' said Andy, 'I think the jury's out as to whether Sir Anthony Cheswell was nuts or a genius.'

'Oh come on!' said Heather. 'The guy spent years trying to persuade everyone that Crumbleton should be a city. On top of that, he had some insane plan to install a railway so that people wouldn't have to walk up the hill.'

'Well, there have definitely been days when I wouldn't have minded a lift from the City Gates up to the top,' said Andy.

'So call Brian and catch a taxi,' said Heather, rolling her eyes.

'But… nothing ever came of it?' said Cath. 'The railway, I mean?'

'Nah,' said Andy, shaking his head, 'just like most of his ideas. He was the one who established the museum though, and he installed the bells in the castle tower too.'

'There are bells up there?' said Cath. 'I don't think I've heard them yet!'

'Well no, you probably wouldn't have,' said Heather, 'they're not exactly "magnificent" like the tourist guidebook claims. They just make a bit of a dull *thunk*… but you're lucky if they do it the right number of times—'

'Or anywhere near the hour,' said Andy. 'I like them, though. They're part of Crumbleton's charm.'

'You *would* say that,' said Heather. 'I guess that's because you're part of Crumbleton's charm too!'

Andy stuck his tongue out at his sister, and Cath laughed. He had a sudden, mad desire to keep making her do that for the rest of his life.

'Anyway,' said Heather, 'Cheswell's part in the town's history tends to get glossed over a bit.'

'But why?' said Cath, clearly intrigued.

'Well,' said Heather, 'he had all these grand plans, but they all ended up being half-arsed because he kept running out of money. Everything he tried to achieve was done on a budget. I mean… look at the City Gates.'

'I love them,' said Andy. 'It's all those little quirks that make Crumbleton unique. I know people always want to make out that the town is ancient - medieval at the very least, and there *are* some seriously old parts like the cobbles outside the museum, but—'

'Oh, not with the stones again!' said Heather, rolling her eyes. 'You know what? On that note, I'm going back to work.'

Andy grinned at his sister as she beat a hasty retreat.

'Don't mind her,' he said to Cath, who was looking mildly alarmed. 'It's a running joke.'

'Er… okay,' said Cath.

'Anyway, as I was saying… people tend to want Crumbleton to pretend to be something it's not, but there's tons of history here if you know where to look.'

'Well thanks, it's definitely good to hear some of the

history,' said Cath. 'Especially the bits that aren't in the books. I've clearly got a lot to learn about the place.'

'I've always found the best way to learn about a town is through its people.' Andy quickly closed his mouth feeling like a total plonker. What was he doing, lecturing a curator on how to do her job, when his job was mending cobbles and cutting grass?! 'Sorry! I don't know what I'm talking about.'

'Yes, you do,' said Cath. 'I totally agree. I—watch out behind you!'

Andy turned to see the first car of the day trundling up the hill towards them.

'Damn,' he muttered. 'I'd better finish up here and get out of the way before someone tries to illegally park on me.'

'Well, thank you for the company,' said Cath. 'Will you say thanks to Heather for the fruit slice too? I didn't get to pay—'

'It's on me,' said Andy quickly. 'Like I said, it's your welcome to Crumbleton cake.'

'Oh, but—'

'But nothing,' said Andy with a smile. 'There'll be plenty of chances to return the favour.'

'Sounds like a plan,' said Cath.

'And if you need a hand with anything, I'm on that list of numbers of yours. Andy Morgan.'

'In that case, Mr Morgan,' said Cath with a warm smile that made his knees do something funny, 'I'll probably speak to you in about ten minutes.'

CHAPTER 7

CATH

'It's a miracle!'

Cath didn't know who she was talking to. She was working alone in the empty museum... but she couldn't let this moment pass without marking it somehow.

Her first box of the day was officially empty!

Day two at her new job was going well so far. Of course, it helped that she'd actually been able to let herself in without having to call for assistance. Andy's wiggle-trick with the old key seemed to be a sure thing. It also helped that—unlike yesterday—she knew exactly what she was walking into. The museum was still an absolute disaster zone, but at least she was prepared for it. Plus, she now had a bit of a plan.

The previous day had been... overwhelming.

After leaving Andy and Heather at the bakery, Cath had returned to the museum, but she didn't manage to get much done. She'd found it impossible to figure out where to start. By the time lunch rolled around, she'd called it a day and headed back to the flat.

After edging between her own piles of cardboard boxes, she'd flopped down onto the patchwork sofa and indulged in an afternoon nap. As if by magic, she'd woken up with a plan of attack for the museum. A plan that was simple and straightforward. She'd dug out her journal and scrawled it down so that she couldn't forget its brilliance.

Now, the torn-out page was folded in Cath's back pocket like a talisman against getting overwhelmed. Reaching for it, she pulled the page out and unfolded it carefully.

One box at a time.

'So far, so good!' she said with a smile, returning the note back to her pocket for safekeeping.

Grabbing the pair of scissors she'd brought with her from the flat, Cath broke down the empty box so that she could stash the cardboard near the door, ready for recycling. It felt ceremonious, somehow.

'Only about three hundred thousand more to go,' she chuckled, carting it towards the entrance and leaning it up against the wall.

Cath glanced longingly at the door. She'd closed it on her way in, but now she was tempted to open it up again. She could do with letting a fresh breeze in to combat the fusty smell of stale air and newly disturbed junk.

Wiping her hands on her jeans, Cath grabbed the heavy old door and pulled. Beams of golden sunlight full of dancing dust promptly flooded through the gap.

'Fresh air!' cheered Cath.

Hmm… maybe it wasn't the best idea to leave the door wide open while she worked, though? But this was Crumbleton, not London. She was sure she'd be completely safe. That said, she wouldn't put it past curious visitors to just wander in… and she definitely wasn't ready for that yet.

Turning to search for a solution, Cath's eyes came to rest on an old plastic school chair balanced precariously on top of a stack of suitcases.

'Perfect!'

She grabbed it and propped it in the doorway with its back to the outside world. There. That should at least slow down any unwanted visitors!

A bit of fresh air was such a simple pleasure, but there was no way Cath would have even considered doing such a thing back at the gallery. For one thing—the air in the capital wasn't exactly what you'd call fresh! But there was also the safety side of things to consider.

The gallery had boasted a sophisticated alarm system, which was a total nightmare to deal with. Even when they were open, there had been a security guard posted outside the door, and they'd had a wealth of panic buttons to choose from too.

'Ridiculous,' muttered Cath, weaving her way back through the box maze to where she'd been working. Why anyone in their right mind would want to burgle the gallery was beyond her. Sure, some of the splodgy paintings and sculptures had been worth hundreds of thousands of pounds, but just the idea of someone trying to half-inch a chunk of metal that looked like someone's first welding lesson was just... funny.

Even though she'd worked there for years, Cath didn't think she was going to miss the gallery for a second. Sure, this was different, and it was *definitely* going to be quite a challenge... but it could be a lot of fun, too.

Patting the note in her pocket again, Cath smiled. *One box at a time.* It was time for the next one.

Rolling up her sleeves, she eyeballed the next likely candidate and flipped open the flaps. It was a box full of empty jam jars along with several dozen rusty lids.

Cath grinned. If she made this into a game, the time would fly by. She'd have three categories: Display. Store. Dispose.

Easy peasy!

'Dispose!' she cheered, hauling the box into her arms and tucking her hands under the bottom just in case it decided to fall apart on her way back to the door.

'Hello?'

Cath jumped, let out a little squeak of surprise and fumbled with the box. The jars clanked ominously as she hugged the whole lot tightly to stop it from slipping.

'Andy!' she gasped.

'Sorry, sorry!' he said, looking mortified. 'I didn't mean to make you jump, but the door was open. I thought I heard you talking to someone?'

Cath winced. 'Just myself!'

'Woman after my own heart,' said Andy, holding out a takeaway cup. 'Anyway, swap you?'

'You do realise you're in serious danger right now, don't you?' said Cath, relaxing slightly as her eyes rested on his strong, rough fingers curling around the cardboard cup.

Don't be weird. Don't stare!

'Danger?' said Andy. 'How?'

'Start bringing me treats and I'll get used to it,' said Cath, smiling at him.

'Well... that doesn't sound so bad,' said Andy with a shrug. 'I wasn't sure what to bring you. Is a latte alright?'

'Pretty perfect right now!' said Cath. 'I think I've already had about a dozen too many cups of tea this morning. Thank you... for thinking of me.'

'Of course,' said Andy easily, setting the cup down on a ledge so that he could take the box from her. 'Anyway, the drink gave me an excuse to check you hadn't been buried alive under a pile of boxes.'

'Still alive and kicking,' said Cath, taking a grateful swig of hot coffee. 'And refuelled, thanks to you!' she added, saluting him with the cup.

Andy grinned at her. 'Where were you heading with this?'

'Near the door somewhere,' she said. 'I'm making a pile of things to be recycled. I'm sorting everything into three categories—display, store, dispose.'

'And this is in the dispose pile?' he said with interest.

'I think I can safely recycle a box of old jam jars without the fear of accidentally chucking away anything of historical importance,' she said.

'You sure?!' said Andy, his eyes going wide.

'I... well... I was, but...' spluttered Cath, instantly second-guessing herself. Was she being too gung-ho with the town's treasures?

'Relax,' chuckled Andy. 'I was joking. I'll get rid of this for you.'

'Cheers!' said Cath, waving him off. 'And thanks again for the coffee.'

'I'm not planning on going anywhere just yet... unless you want me to clear off?' said Andy. 'I've got a couple of hours free if you'd like an extra pair of hands?'

'Well, I'm not going to say no to a bit of free labour!' said Cath.

'Cool,' said Andy. 'Be right back.'

Cath turned away from him, clutching her drink

and doing her best not to start overthinking things. Part of her really wanted to prove that she could conquer this new challenge on her own. After being under her ex's thumb and subject to his annoying whims the whole time she'd supposedly been in charge of the gallery, she needed to know that she could stand on her own two feet.

But... that didn't mean she had to be pig-headed, did it? She liked Andy. He seemed like a kind, thoughtful guy, and he was easy company. Besides, clearing out enough rubbish so that she had some space to start work in earnest was a priority... and something she'd achieve a lot faster with some help.

Of course, it didn't hurt that Andy improved the view no-end.

'Erm... Cath? Where are you?' called Andy.

'Here!' Cath laughed. 'Behind the boxes!'

'That really helps,' said Andy, appearing around the corner, his eyes crinkled with laughter. 'This place is ninety-nine per cent boxes!'

Yup, definitely a very fine view!

Andy had stripped out of the top part of his overalls, and he'd tied the arms around his waist. Underneath, he was wearing a soft grey tee shirt... and Cath would swear she could see the outline of defined muscles through the cotton. His arms were bare and tanned and...

'Big,' she sighed.

'Pardon?' said Andy.

Cath widened her eyes. *Oh no no no!*

'Big… erm… mess!' she amended hastily, tearing her eyes off him and nodding at the tallest tower of boxes.

'Yeah. So… where do you want me to start?' said Andy, folding his arms and practically making Cath swoon in the process. Somehow, she just about managed to stay upright.

Unfortunately, the same couldn't be said for the leaning tower of boxes, and they chose that exact moment to give way.

'Watch out!' gasped Cath, leaping towards Andy and shoving him backwards, out of their path.

'Hi!' he said, blinking at her in surprise.

Cath was suddenly aware that she had him pinned at an odd angle against a table piled high with dusty lampshades.

'Nice reflexes,' he said. 'Thanks for that!'

'You're… erm… you're welcome,' said Cath.

Her hands were resting on his chest… and she'd been right. He was solid underneath his soft tee shirt. And warm. And he smelled nice too.

Cath swallowed and pulled away from him.

'Sorry,' she muttered.

'Don't apologise for saving me from that lot,' he said, straightening up and peering at the crumpled heap of cardboard, broken glass and random rubbish all over the floor. 'I had no idea working in a museum could be so dangerous. Maybe I should have brought my hard hat!'

'Maybe,' said Cath vaguely. She blinked stupidly, trying to pull herself together and get her mind off Andy's body and back onto the job. 'Erm, I meant to ask… why do you have to wear a hard hat anyway?'

'Health and safety gone a bit mad,' said Andy with a shrug. 'Mind you, I've been glad of it these last few weeks.'

'Why's that?' said Cath, not meeting his eye as she nudged a couple of bits of glass with her foot.

'Flying cola cubes,' chuckled Andy.

'Huh?'

'Kids,' said Andy.

'Oh,' said Cath.

'So… anyway… where are we going to start?' said Andy.

'Well, this seems like as good a place as any,' she said, pointing at the recent box-slide and still avoiding his eye. 'Just watch out for any more avalanches!'

CHAPTER 8

ANDY

'This?' said Andy, striking a pose to catch Cath's attention.

Cath turned and looked straight towards his empty hands.

'What?' she said, looking confused. Then she spotted the lampshade he'd put on his head and was now wearing as a fetching, tasselled hat.

'As much as it suits you,' she said, her face creasing with laughter, 'it's got a huge tear down the back, so I think that can go in the *dispose* pile.'

'The dispose mountain, you mean?' said Andy, removing the lampshade and tossing it towards the heap of stuff that would be off to the local tip the minute he could find someone to lend Cath a van for the job.

Andy had noticed that she'd become more decisive and a bit more ruthless with her decisions as they worked their way through box after box. The town had certainly been generous with their donations... but their historical value was rather lacking.

To be fair to Cath though, anything that could be rehomed or recycled had been added to a different pile. Andy had no doubt that she'd make sure it would all find the right homes eventually.

All in all, he was having far more fun than the task warranted. After her initial nervousness about getting stuck in "in case she got it wrong", Cath had led the way with gusto.

There had been plenty of laughs along the way, especially when they'd come across a suitcase full of comedy sunglasses. They'd spent a good ten minutes trying the stars and heart-shaped frames on for size. That case had made its way into the "display" pile... even though Cath had admitted that she had no idea how she was ever going to use them.

'What about this?' said Cath, popping an old naval captain's hat onto her head.

'Erm... well... I guess if you plan on doing any nautical-themed displays, it might come in handy. And it *might* have some history to it,' said Andy.

'It's a keeper, then,' said Cath.

'Yeah... though you might want to take it off,' said Andy, struggling to keep a smile off his face.

'Why?' said Cath with an exaggerated pout. 'Doesn't it suit me?'

'Oh, it definitely does,' said Andy slowly. In fact, she

looked decidedly cute in it, but... 'I just think you might want to wipe that splodge of ancient seagull poop off it before it goes on display... or on your head!'

'Eww, gross!' said Cath, grabbing the hat and whipping it off before inspecting it at arm's length. 'Nice!' she laughed, noting the ominous white stain.

'It could be paint?' said Andy.

'Nope, I think you were right with your first guess!' laughed Cath, popping it on the "display" pile, nonetheless.

Andy checked the bottom of the cardboard box he'd been emptying for any lurking leftovers, and then with a little cheer, he turned it over to slice the tape neatly with a pair of scissors.

'That's another empty!' he said triumphantly.

'Phew. Well... we're getting somewhere,' said Cath, putting her hands on her hips and stretching her back.

'The joys of teamwork, eh,' said Andy, dusting his hands together.

'Yep. And here's another empty,' said Cath, bending down and removing an old KitKat tin from the bottom of the box she'd been working on.

'Chuck it here,' said Andy, holding out his hand for the box.

Cath tossed it to him and Andy broke it down. Bundling all the cardboard up together, he carted it over to the already impressive stack beside the door.

'What's up?' he said curiously, noticing that Cath was still staring at the floor when he came back.

'How long have we been at it?' she said, glancing at him.

Andy shook back his sleeve to look at his watch. 'About… two hours,' he said. 'Why?'

'Because it's taken us two hours to make our way down through the layers to our very first patch of newly cleared carpet,' said Cath.

'Blimey!' chuckled Andy, glancing at the spot Cath was pointing at. 'I always thought the carpet in here was a kind of motheaten grey!'

'Erm… try dark navy,' said Cath, scrunching up her nose. 'That gives us some idea how long that stack of boxes has been sitting there!'

'And how long it's been since anyone ran a hoover around this place,' said Andy.

'I'll add it to my to-do list,' said Cath, running her fingers through her hair. 'Though I haven't actually spotted a hoover yet.'

'You know what this means, right?' said Andy.

'That it's going to take ages to get this place open to the public?' said Cath, looking like she was slowly deflating.

'Nope,' said Andy, shaking his head. 'It means it's time for us to celebrate.'

'What—just because we uncovered our first bit of carpet?' said Cath.

'Exactly!' said Andy. 'Celebrate the small wins. Besides, it's lunchtime. My treat, if you fancy it?'

He crossed his fingers behind his back and watched

as Cath stared around her at the piles of chaos. They were marginally more organised than when they'd started a few hours ago, but in reality, they'd barely scratched the surface. Andy could see that Cath was loathe to take a break, but she also looked tired and overwhelmed.

'A bite to eat and something to drink, and you'll be ready to jump straight back in,' he said, doing his best to sound encouraging. 'You never know—Heather might have some fruit slices left.'

'Okay, those were the magic words!' said Cath, turning to smile at him. 'You win.'

'I thought the mention of a fruit slice might sway you,' he said. 'Let's go!'

∽

Andy felt like a bit of an idiot as the pair of them wandered down the high street towards the bakery… mainly because he couldn't wipe the broad smile off his face.

It was odd. He usually took a while to feel truly comfortable around new people, but Cath was so easy to chat to that he felt like he'd known her for years. They'd worked side-by-side all morning, and there hadn't been many silences… and the ones there *had* been had felt friendly.

'Blimey,' said Cath, dodging around a family of tourists who'd stopped in the middle of the pavement to take selfies. 'I had no idea Crumbleton got this busy.'

'This?' said Andy. 'This is nothing. Seriously. There are days when it feels like there must be a music festival happening in town or something. You get elbowed and jostled just wandering down to Bendall's for a pint of milk. I'll have to show you where all the shortcuts are—they'll save your sanity on a busy summer's day.'

'Shortcuts?' said Cath.

'Yep,' he nodded. 'You can pretty much get from the top of town all the way down to the City Gates without having to deal with the high street, as long as you don't mind navigating dozens of steps!'

'Good to know,' said Cath. 'I'll take you up on that offer at some point.'

'Deal. Any time,' said Andy. 'But right now... let's get some lunch!'

He paused to peer through the bakery window and Cath came to stand next to him. The hairs on his arm promptly stood on end.

'Your poor sister,' said Cath. 'She's rammed in there!'

'Trust me, she's in her element,' said Andy, grinning at Heather through the glass as his sister turned her wide, slightly wild eyes to the pair of them. There were at least a dozen people in the queue, waiting to be served.

'I'm not sure the fact that she's mouthing "save me"

through the window means she's in her element!' chuckled Cath.

'Okay, you might have a point,' said Andy.

'Should we go in and help her?' said Cath.

'Hell no!' said Andy, shaking his head. 'Seriously. I tried it once. Never again. I just got in her way. She doesn't really want any help... she'll have it all under control.'

'Fair enough,' said Cath.

'Come on, let's leave her to it,' said Andy. 'We'll see if the café's any quieter. We'll grab lunch in there and then pop back when Heather's dealt with that lot.'

Andy led the way a bit further down the hill and then held the café door open for Cath.

'There's a table over there,' she said, pointing towards the back. 'That family's just leaving.'

'Quick, let's grab it before anyone else beats us to it!' said Andy. 'Mabel will come over to us when she's got a sec.'

The pair of them hurried through the packed café, dodged around the family heading for the exit, and slid straight into the chairs at their newly vacated table.

'That was a bit of luck,' said Andy, gathering together the empty cups and plates and stacking them at the edge of the table. 'Well spotted!'

'Just in time too,' said Cath, nodding back towards the door. 'Look, someone else just came in and there's nowhere for her to sit.'

Andy glanced over. 'That's Caroline Cook!' he said.

'You don't mind if she joins us, do you? We've got a couple of spare seats, and it seems a bit mean to hog the extra spaces.'

'Fine by me,' said Cath with an easy shrug.

Andy waved vigorously to catch Caroline's attention and then beckoned her over.

'Join us?'

'Lifesavers!' breathed Caroline as she slid into one of the empty seats. 'You guys sure you don't mind? I don't want to be a gooseberry!'

Andy snorted and then noticed that Cath had just turned that remarkably pretty shade of pink again.

'We're not...' she stuttered.

'You're grand!' said Andy quickly, wanting to cover Cath's discomfort. 'Caroline, this is Cath Walker—she's our new curator.'

'Cath!' said Caroline, her face splitting into a wide smile. 'I was hoping we'd bump into each other sooner rather than later. I gave the museum a little mention in the paper last week—just to let everyone know it's due to reopen soon, now that we've got you in town!'

'You did?' said Cath, sounding slightly panicked.

Andy smiled at her, doing his best to look reassuring. Now that he'd seen the state the museum was in, he couldn't blame her for looking worried. The idea of reopening to the public anytime soon was almost laughable at this point.

'I have to say,' said Caroline, ploughing on as her

eyes skimmed down the laminated café menu, 'I think you're really brave to take on the job.'

'I'm not sure about brave,' said Cath. 'I mean, the place is in a bit of a state, and there's loads of rubbish to get rid of, but it's nothing I can't handle.'

'Good for you!' said Caroline, with an approving nod. 'To be honest, I'm surprised it hasn't been closed for good by this point.'

'Ah now, don't say that,' said Andy uncomfortably.

'Well, haven't you thought exactly the same thing?' said Caroline. 'It doesn't get many visitors... though maybe that's a good thing considering it's a giant health and safety disaster waiting to happen.'

'Well, it's not had proper staff for a long time,' said Andy.

He was aware that he was starting to sound a bit defensive, just like he always did when anyone dared to criticise his beloved town. Caroline did have a point though.

'No,' said Caroline. 'That's true, Cath's post was vacant for donkey's yonks. Problem is, there's not much in the way of budget for the council to keep it open, is there? And if it doesn't prove itself...' she trailed off.

'Wait,' said Cath. 'What do you mean, there's not much in the budget? I mean, they've hired me...'

Caroline bit her lip and glanced uncomfortably at Andy. He let out a long sigh. This was the last thing poor Cath needed to hear. She'd only just started, and there was a vast mountain of work for her to do before she even had a hope of reopening. Still, maybe it was better that she knew what she was up against.

'The council's broke,' said Andy steadily.

'Yeah,' Caroline nodded, 'very. The only reason the curator role was still being advertised is because they've still got the money available from last year's pot. It's ringfenced, you see? They couldn't use it for anything else. I'm betting they would have if they could have, though!'

Andy winced as he watched the bad news land, one blow at a time. He could almost see the weight of what they were telling her landing on Cath's shoulders.

'I'm... I'm, erm... guessing this is all news to you?' said Caroline.

Cath nodded silently.

'Well, it's better that you know,' she said, her face serious. 'As far as I've been told, they've got enough in the pot to cover your salary for a year, but there's only about six months' worth of finances left to run the place. We're just talking about the basics like keeping the lights on—not all the repairs that need seeing to.'

'I had no idea things were this bad,' said Andy, shaking his head. 'I mean I knew things at the council were tight, but...'

'The only reason *you* still have a job is that you cover so many different roles, they can't work out which bits they can afford to cut!' said Caroline, trying to catch Mabel's eye as she zoomed around, serving the heaving tables.

'Well, that's comforting,' muttered Andy. He was only half-listening. Cath was now looking pale and deflated across from him as she pretended to peruse her menu.

'So,' she said slowly, not lifting her eyes, 'you're saying I might be out of a job in six months—a year, tops?'

'Don't quote me on it,' said Caroline nodding. 'If you want my advice, you might want to put a rocket under Ruth and make her give you the actual figures. At least then you'll know exactly what you've got to work with… or not, as the case may be.'

'I will,' said Cath quietly. 'Thanks.'

CHAPTER 9

CATH

The walk back up the hill from the café to the museum felt like climbing Everest instead of a gentle amble up the picturesque cobbles. Cath felt like her feet were encased in blocks of lead—but she knew the sudden heaviness in her limbs and desire to climb under a blanket in a darkened room had nothing to do with being tired.

Lunch had been far from the fun, happy break she'd been expecting. In fact, she felt a bit like the tenuous grasp she had on her new reality had just come under fire from a bunch of pipe bombs.

Cath didn't blame Caroline for bringing the subject up. In fact, she had a feeling the pair of them would get on like a house on fire… when the woman in question wasn't doling out more home truths than Cath had been expecting over her cheese and ham toastie.

To say that it had left her feeling a bit demoralised was the understatement of the century. And frankly, didn't she have every right to feel like that? It looked like the council had been anything but straight with her during the interview process.

The burning question now was, where did it leave her?

Living in a new town, in a strange flat piled high with boxes – that was where. Cath's new job might look like a dream on paper, but in reality, it looked like that particular piece of paper might be on fire.

'I knew it was too good to be true,' she sighed, mooching past the florist and the antiques shop with downcast eyes and an even more downcast heart. She couldn't believe she might be job hunting again in just a few short months.

Blowing out a long, slow breath, Cath slotted the big stupid key back into the big stupid lock and gave it a big stupid wiggle.

The wave of possibility she'd been riding all morning had well and truly vanished. Now she was left with a queasy kind of sinking sensation in the pit of her stomach, and very little energy or enthusiasm left to attack the next round of junk waiting for her inside.

Cath dashed inside, flicked on the lights, and then headed back to the door and slammed it shut. She wasn't in the mood for any unexpected visitors this afternoon. Still, she didn't want to get a reputation as a grumpy baggage and she *definitely* didn't have it in her to be a smiling ray of sunshine if any of the locals happened to pop in to say hello. As for the dithering gaggles of tourists...

'Better to shut them out!' muttered Cath, turning the key in the lock for good measure.

There. Now at least she could be a grump without risking an audience. As much as she'd enjoyed Andy's company earlier, she was glad that he'd had to disappear off after lunch to deal with one of his many maintenance jobs. She needed some time to digest what she'd just learned, and she *really* didn't want to end up taking the bad news out on him.

There wasn't much point in sulking though, was there? Ruth wouldn't be back in the country for a couple of weeks, so getting to the bottom of the museum's funding and finding out the future of her job was going to have to wait.

'Right,' said Cath in a loud, purposeful voice, hoping that it might trick her brain into thinking that everything was hunky-dory.

It didn't work.

If she was being honest, Cath had no idea what to do next. Unfortunately, it looked like the magic of the plan in her back pocket had worn off over lunch.

Picking her way through the newly sorted piles and stacks of boxes looking for some inspiration, Cath was surprised at how much the pair of them had managed to achieve in just one morning. There was certainly a lot more space to move around, and they'd even managed to shift most of the piles away from the front of the glass cabinet that held the tennis equipment.

In fact, if she just moved that bundle of old newspapers and the heap of what looked like old theatre curtains out of the way, she might even be able to get the doors open for a closer look. It would be nice to see if there was anything interesting in the lower half of the cabinet.

Grabbing the string that was looped around the bundle of newspapers, she dragged them out of the way. She'd take them over to the pile of recycling later. Cath shifted her attention to the heap of red, velvet curtain. She gingerly took hold of a handful of the grubby fabric and tugged.

A plume of dust rose in the air, and Cath had to pause to sneeze.

And sneeze.

And sneeze again.

'Enough already!' she muttered, rubbing her nose with the back of her hand in an attempt to stop the explosions.

'Okay, change of plan,' she muttered, eyeballing the curtains. There was no way she was getting her face too close to them again. Instead, she started to nudge the pile of fabric out of the way with her foot until the glass doors were clear.

'That'll do,' she sniffed.

Leaning forward, she gave the dusty glass door a gentle tug.

'Locked? Are you serious?!' she laughed. Somehow, she couldn't imagine anyone wanting to make off with an old tennis net and a few moulting balls. 'Damnit... now what?'

Patting her jeans pockets, Cath felt for the smaller bunch of keys that Ruth had sent her with the Welcome Pack. They had to be for something in the building, didn't they? With any luck...

Pulling the little ring of ancient keys from her back pocket, Cath flipped through them, looking for a likely candidate. The lock looked like it was made of brass.

'This one?' she murmured, not holding out much hope that the very first one she tried would actually work.

'Eureka!'

It turned easily and the door swung open with no effort at all.

'Okay that was too easy,' she muttered, peering inside.

The grubby sweatbands and old shorts didn't look any more appealing than they had with the doors closed. She'd been right about the net being decidedly tangled... and the balls were more motheaten than she'd originally thought. In fact, they were practically bald.

Crouching down, Cath started to inspect the lower levels of the display case that had been hidden behind all the junk.

'So, this is where all the fluff went!' she muttered, reaching in and gingerly shifting a cloud of yellow fibres that had clearly once belonged to the bald balls on the shelf above.

Underneath, there were a couple of wooden-cased rackets that had probably been originally used as a backdrop before they'd tumble into the rest of the mess. Cath shifted them aside, only to reveal a couple of rusty old cogs that looked like they might belong to the ancient piece of machinery behind the cabinet. They certainly bore splatters of matching white paint.

'I wonder...' she said, turning them over. Could the machine possibly have been used to paint the court lines?

Cath shrugged and peered right to the back, only to find a velvet plinth. The green cloth had faded around the edges, but there was a circular patch of dark green right on the top—an echo of something that had sat there for years before being moved.

Lost? Stolen? Sold? It was anyone's guess!

Right in the middle of this circle sat a scrap of paper —curled and yellowing at the edges. Cath could just make out a few letters of faint, spidery handwriting. It felt crispy between her fingertips as she reached for it and then gingerly eased back the curled edges to read it.

Sir Anthony Cheswell Cup – loaned to the antiques shop.

'Which antiques shop?!' said Cath. She could only assume the note was referring to the one next door... but that was just a guess. Probably a decent guess though, right?

'Well, there's only one way to find out!' she said, popping the paper back on its plinth and straightening up again with some difficulty.

There wasn't any point in locking the case back up. Cath would have to empty it anyway to clean and rearrange its contents at the very least... though it was likely that process would involve a big black bin-liner somewhere along the way!

'Anthony Cheswell, Anthony Cheswell,' she muttered, heading back towards the door. The name was familiar. Wasn't that the eccentric businessman Heather and Andy had been talking about? The one who'd built the Dolphin and Anchor?

Cath shrugged. She couldn't remember... but she was definitely going to investigate. Somehow, she didn't fancy diving into yet more boxes of junk. Getting to the bottom of this little Crumbleton mystery was far more appealing right now!

Pushing the museum door open a crack, Cath checked the coast was clear and that she wasn't about to walk straight out into a crowd of visitors. Then she sidled out onto the cobbles and quickly locked up behind her before jogging the couple steps to the antiques shop. There, she paused to have her first proper look at the window display.

'Bingo!' she said in surprise.

Well, it hadn't taken much to solve the mystery of the whereabouts of the cup – it was right there in front of her! It was huge and silver, and the name of the competition was engraved across its slightly tarnished curves.

Around its heavy, circular black base, there were several smaller silver shields, each one engraved with the names of dozens of winners, along with a year. One of the shields was only half full, and the last name on the list was E. Barker. It was dated 1988.

Cath hot-footed it towards the door and excitedly pushed her way inside.

'Can I help you?!'

The slightly scary demand brought her up short. There was nothing warm or welcoming about it. In fact, it was the kind of voice that would cut through a thunderstorm and miles of thick sea fog.

'Erm... hi!' said Cath, her voice sounding weedy by comparison. She smiled at the woman glaring at her from the other side of the shop. Cath's first impression of her was something along the lines of "larger than life". From her booming voice to her *interesting* dress sense – an orange waistcoat over a floral shirt and green and white striped culottes – there was nothing in the least bit subtle about her. She was eyeballing Cath suspiciously from behind a pair of old-fashioned men's glasses—the kind that were black on the top and clear at the bottom.

'I'm... erm... I'm Cath?'

'You don't sound too sure about that!' proclaimed the woman.

Cath cleared her throat and decided to try again... this time with a bit more certainty.

'Yep – definitely sure,' she said. 'I'm Cath Walker. I'm the new curator next door.' She paused again, not entirely sure whether she wanted to ask about the trophy after all. Maybe she could just wimp out and slink back to the museum.

'Geraldine Scott,' announced the woman.

'It's nice to meet you.' Cath held out her hand, but Geraldine didn't take it. Instead, she eyed it with suspicion and then crossed her arms over her ample bosom.

'So, I guess you're here about the cup?'

Well... at least that made things easier. Now Cath didn't have to figure out how to broach the subject!

'Yes, I—'

'I meant to give it back when the last version of you left,' said Geraldine, sounding defensive, 'but it's a lovely piece of silverware, and it's important to the town. Anyway, I gave it pride of place in the window... and if I'm honest, I don't really think about it much.'

Cath nodded. The antiques shop was a right little

Aladdin's cave. There were shelves from floor to ceiling, and they were all full to overflowing. Some of them were bowing ominously under the weight of curios, and Cath couldn't help but wonder how often one of them gave up the will and went crashing down along with several hundred pounds worth of stock.

As for the window display, it looked like you'd pretty much have to send a mountaineering team out on an exhibition just to reach it, so she wasn't exactly surprised that Geraldine didn't think about it too often!

'I don't have it for sale if that's what you're thinking,' huffed Geraldine.

'Oh no!' said Cath, shaking her head. 'I didn't, I mean I…'

'I get it out of there twice a year to empty out the dead flies and give it a bit of a polish. I mean… it's worth the effort. It's part of the town's history—and who's going to see it in the museum?' she paused for effect. 'No one, that's who! The place is a shambles.'

Cath felt herself bristling slightly, though she couldn't imagine why. After all, it wasn't her who'd been responsible for letting the place slide into such a state. But still… it was her territory now. At least, it was until the council ran out of cash.

'Well… I'm here to change all that,' she said, squaring her shoulders.

'Hmm,' said Geraldine, raising an eyebrow. 'Well, I

know what the paper said, but I can't see you getting that place open in the next few weeks.'

Watch me!

The words might not have come out of her mouth, but Cath felt the lingering sense of desperation that had been haunting her since lunchtime disappear. Instead, it was replaced by a steely resolve. It felt... unexpectedly good.

'Either way, I'll be needing the cup back,' said Cath, lifting her chin.

'Got something sporty planned?' said Geraldine.

'You know... I might just have,' said Cath, making a snap decision.

'Well, feel free to pick my brain anytime,' said Geraldine. Her voice was still loud enough to set the silverware on the shelves ringing, but it had definitely softened to a degree. 'I hate to say this, but I was at the last game that cup was awarded at.'

'You were?' said Cath.

'I was. Of course, I was a young whippersnapper back then – but I still remember it. Fantastic match... and there were these bowls of amazing strawberries. Locally grown. Sweet and juicy and covered in cream...'

Cath smiled and nodded along as Geraldine waxed lyrical. After about ten minutes without managing to get another word in edgeways, she began to surreptitiously edge back towards the shop door.

'I just need to...' she muttered, tapping her watch

and stepping back onto the street as Geraldine finally paused to breathe.

'Of course, of course,' said Geraldine, flapping two meaty hands at her. 'I'll dig the cup out for you. It might take me a little while though.'

Cath nodded her thanks, still backing away. 'I'll come back for it!'

CHAPTER 10

ANDY

Andy tipped the little green can and guided the trickle of fuel carefully into the tank of the ancient lawnmower.

'There you go, old girl,' he murmured. 'I bought you a drink... so you're going to behave for me now, aren't you?'

The mower didn't answer. Obviously.

Rolling his eyes at himself, Andy peeked over his shoulder to check there was no one around to witness him talking to the decrepit, rusty machine. Thankfully, there wasn't another soul in sight. The sunlit, slightly overgrown garden of the Dolphin and Anchor was mercifully empty.

For some reason, he hadn't been able to get this place out of his head since Cath had asked him about Crumbleton's tennis-playing history. Maybe it was simply because it was long overdue for some of his attention. Or maybe... maybe it would make a nice place to bring a new friend on a late summer's evening.

'Maybe,' said Andy with a shrug, turning his attention back to the mower.

He screwed the cap back onto the fuel tank and gave the flaking red paint a gentle pat before straightening up. Now all he had to do was cross his fingers that a full tank of fuel and a fresh glug of oil would put the old thing in a good enough mood to actually start.

It was an ongoing battle of wills between him and this mower... and the machine usually won. He didn't mind in the slightest, though. He loved tinkering around to get it running. In his opinion, it was worth the extra care and attention—it did a lovely job when it finally deigned to rumble into action.

A relic from the 1950s, the mower had lived in the shed behind the kitchens since before the hotel was even a hotel. Andy knew that Fergus, the owner, would have replaced it a million times over by now if it wasn't for the bargain they'd struck several years ago. If Fergus wanted Andy to cut the grass for him, then Andy wanted to do the job with the beautiful old mower.

As far as Andy knew, he was the only person in town who really knew how to make it run... and he was fine with that. Sure, cherishing a special bond with an antique piece of machinery might make him a bit of an odd-bod in some people's eyes – but as luck would have it, he was fine with that too!

Glancing around the garden again, Andy rolled his sleeves up. It was going to take a bit more work than usual to get things under control this time around. He hadn't been able to cut the grass for weeks—it had simply been too wet.

It wasn't just the grass that had sprung up, either. The rainy start to the summer, followed by the recent warm spell, meant that the shrubs around the edges had run rampant, stretching their bushy branches out as though they were all trying to prove a point.

'Actually, I think I'd better start you on a higher setting!' he muttered, kneeling down again and shifting a lever so that the mower would leave the grass slightly longer—at least for the first cut. If he went too short too fast, the old machine would clog up in seconds, and he'd end up spending most of the day hoicking clumps of gooed-up greenery from its innards.

Andy was already resigned to the fact that it was going to take him a couple of repeated laps to get the lawn back down to a more manageable length. It was hard to believe that it had once been a beautifully manicured tennis court. He'd been thinking about that ever since Cath had asked about it. He'd seen photographs of what it used to look like back in the day—all neat stripes, with carefully painted lines and a pristine white net strung across the middle.

Of course, he knew exactly where the posts for the

net used to slot into the ground because he had to swerve to avoid the holes every time he visited. By this point, they were easy enough to spot because there were two identical tufts of extra-long grass on either side of the lawn that never got chopped.

No one at the hotel called it "the tennis court" anymore… probably because Fergus had decided to put a stop to it to discourage the local kids from turning up with their rackets and annoying the guests.

If the old photographs he'd seen were anything to go by, the court hadn't originally been lined by all these mad, overgrown shrubs. Instead, there had been a series of neat, well-tended flower borders—a riot of colour set against a backdrop of hand-painted wooden signs pointing tennis club members to the bar and the changing rooms.

Some of the signs were still there. Andy occasionally caught sight of them, hidden deep behind the overgrown bushes. It was a shame they'd been left out there to rot, but it would take some doing to get at them now!

It really must have been rather wonderful to watch a game of tennis out there, though. Andy could just imagine sitting in the sunshine, watching with a cold drink in his hand.

Even as the thought crossed his mind, a tickle of an idea crept onto Andy's shoulder and whispered into his ear.

What if he could restore it to its former glory?

A little shiver of excitement ran up Andy's spine. He was sure he could convince Fergus to let him spruce the place up a bit more thoroughly than his usual quick grass-chopping mission... especially if he offered to do it for free.

What could be more romantic than a drink on the terrace? Other than the fact that the terrace was long gone, of course – probably dismantled decades ago. But if everything was neatly trimmed... the flower borders planted up... and the grass all short and neat and striped...

Andy was sure the flagstones for the terrace would still be there if he looked. They were probably buried under a layer of turf. Even if the shady roof had long since disappeared, it would make a lovely spot to pop some chairs and tables. A lot of work... but it would be worth it.

'Ready?' said Andy.

The mower didn't answer again. Obviously.

Andy grinned and grabbed the end of the pull cord.

'Right, here we go!' he murmured. He'd get the grass cut just so—stripes and all if he could manage it. Then he'd talk to Fergus about the other bits.

Giving the cord a swift, sure yank, the ancient engine chugged to life on the first attempt. Andy let out a loud whoop of triumph that was instantly drowned out by the machine's grumbling purr as they set off together, carving the first neat—slightly too-long stripe —through the scruffy grass.

Andy automatically swerved around the tuft of grass that marked one of the holes for the net, completely lost in his daydream of strawberries and cream, a cooling drink on a warm, summery evening… and good company.

Maybe… maybe he could ask Cath to join him there for a drink. After he'd done all the work, of course. The smile on his face only got broader as he imagined clinking his glass of Pimm's with hers—their fingers briefly touching.

15 Love.

They'd catch each other's eye and something would pass between them.

30 Love.

They'd put their drinks down and reach for each other across the table, fingers interlacing in the warm sunshine of an early Crumbleton evening.

40 Love.

Whew, where had that come from? Andy hadn't had thoughts like that about anyone for ages. What was this new arrival doing to him?

He shook his head. Was he being ridiculous? Quite possibly. But there was something about Cath that was making him dream of those simple pleasures again.

'Simple, my foot!' he sighed, turning the machine and plodding slowly back the way he'd just come, lining up another stripe and inhaling the fresh, green scent of the newly mown grass.

In Andy's experience, nothing was simple when it came to falling in love. Actually, that wasn't fair. The falling part was simple enough... it was the bit that came afterwards that usually turned out to be complicated. That was when *people* seemed to want him to change.

Change his job, change his clothes, change his home.

Andy shrugged, trying to shake off the tightness that always appeared in his muscles whenever he thought about his ex. She was long, *long* gone by this point... but he still felt hurt that a person he'd loved and trusted more than anyone else in the world had wanted to change him so much. Tara had wanted to *upgrade* him... like an out-of-date mobile phone.

Maybe that was why he was so keen on looking after old things... like the cobbles and this ancient mower. He wanted them to know that they were loved exactly as they were, quirks and all.

'Idiot!' he sighed, shaking his head. Just because that's what *he* wanted more than anything in life...

The mower gave an ominous choking sound, and Andy promptly paused and cut off the engine. Blimey... the grass bin at the back was full already and he'd barely completed the third stripe!

It was just as well that he had the rest of the afternoon free... he had a feeling this job was going to take a bit of doing, especially if he was going to go all-out on the extra bits. Still, it would be worth it. There was something special about Cath, and he wanted to get to know her better.

Andy nodded to himself. Decision made. He'd empty the grass onto the compost heap and then nip inside and ask Fergus's permission to spruce things up a bit more than usual. Then he'd borrow a couple of deckchairs from Crumbleton Sands. That shouldn't be a problem as he maintained them for the council, and always mended the roof of the little hut they were kept in when it got blown off every winter.

'Then comes the really scary bit,' he muttered.

Then he'd have to actually ask Cath out.

CHAPTER 11

CATH

Cath snuggled back into the cushions and let out a happy sigh. It had been another exhausting morning at the museum – and she'd spent it working outwards from the glass cabinet holding the various bits of tennis paraphernalia. After emptying about a dozen boxes—most of which had ended up in the "to be recycled" pile, Cath had decided to slink back to the flat for a spot of lunch.

She might not know Oli very well yet, but Cath could hug the man for leaving behind his beautiful patchwork sofa when he'd moved out. She could see it was going to quickly become her happy place.

After visiting Geraldine in the antiques shop the previous day, Cath hadn't been able to face heading back to the museum again. The news that her job might be temporary had thrown her for a loop, and even though she'd momentarily distracted herself with the mystery of the "missing" Anthony Cheswell cup, finding it in the shop window next door had solved that particular puzzle a little bit too quickly. Besides, after her little chat with Geraldine, Cath's mind had been racing with new possibilities. She'd wanted to give them space to grow, rather than losing them under the piles of rubbish still waiting to be sorted.

Instead, she'd decided to spend some time unpacking at the flat. Making the place more comfortable and homey might have looked counterintuitive to anyone else—given the chance she might have to move out again sooner than expected—but to Cath, it had felt a bit like a defiant act of rebellion. This was her home now, and she was going to make the most of it... even if she didn't get to stay for very long.

All the unpacking and dragging around of furniture to find the perfect spots also meant that the rest of the day had disappeared. When she'd fallen into bed, she'd slept the sleep of the dead.

Still, all the hard work had been worth it. When she'd dragged herself blearily out of bed that morning, it had been heavenly to find herself in a flat that was no longer packed from floor to ceiling with cardboard boxes. The kitchen was sparkling clean and stocked with her favourite cookware, dining sets and cutlery. Plus, her beautiful rainbow mugs were sitting on the counter, ready for her morning cuppa.

In the sitting room, the bookshelves were crammed with her own novels and knickknacks, and her multicoloured rag rug was looking right at home in front of the patchwork sofa.

It had all given Cath the boost she'd needed to face the new day with a smile on her face again, and what was more, the seed of the idea that had germinated the previous day had done some serious growing while she'd occupied her mind elsewhere.

Cath was now determined to find a way to make sure that she turned things around at the museum. It should be right at the heart of the community, not a tatty dumping ground everyone pretended didn't exist. To do that, she needed to buy herself more time there… and stop it from falling down while she pulled it all together. To do that, she was going to need an injection of cash.

Her search through the boxes that morning had been far more focused than the previous couple of days. She was looking for more clues that would help her build on her new idea.

'Question is, am I going to find anything useful in here?' she yawned, settling a heavy photo album in her lap. She'd slipped it into her bag to look through while she was eating her lunch after discovering it at the bottom of a disintegrating box not far from the tennis cabinet. It had been hiding under a layer of yet more empty jam jars, and she'd come very close to dumping the whole lot onto the recycling pile without even checking through it.

Lesson learned!

'Oh wow!' she gasped as she flipped it open to a random page full of sepia photographs of people wearing tennis whites. They were action shots of a match in progress.

Shifting to put her mug of tea down on the nearby coffee table so that she had both hands free to peruse the album, Cath quickly flipped back to the front and let her fingers trace the lettering there. A fine, flowing calligraphy script read:

Sir Anthony Cheswell Cup

Turning the pages carefully, Cath's eyes flicked from one photograph to the next. There were lots of smiles and fancy hats. The players all wore pristine whites and wielded quaint, wooden rackets. It looked like a terrific event if the hundreds of happy faces in the crowd were anything to go by.

The next page showed off shots of picnic tables – laden with bowl after bowl of gleaming strawberries and what looked like pitchers of thick cream, though it was hard to tell in monochrome!

Cath sped up, flipping through the pages, and watching as colour crept into the photographs. The hairstyles and hemlines of the crowd might be changing, but the strawberries, smiles and sunshine remained the same right until the last page... as did the plentiful supply of champers served in beautiful vintage glassware.

As though her body was stealing the frozen bubbles from the photographs, Cath felt a curious tingle creeping up her legs from her toes. It was a similar feeling to when she'd ploughed into Andy in the museum to save him from that falling pile of boxes— a sensation of possibility and excitement.

'But... would it work now?' she muttered, coming to the end of the album and gently closing its covers.

Something inside her was telling her that this was important. Against all odds, she had a feeling the way to start breathing life back into the museum lay between these pages.

But... she wouldn't be able to do it without help. After all, she was a newcomer, and even though all of the people she'd met so far had been lovely, she didn't know nearly enough people to get something like this off the ground.

'But I know someone who does!' she said, rolling off the sofa with a bump and scrambling to her feet.

Suddenly, all her aches from shifting furniture the day before were gone, replaced by the delicious fizz of possibility that had now spread from her legs to every inch of her body.

Grabbing her bag, Cath popped the old album

carefully back inside. Then, pausing just long enough to gulp the dregs of her cup of tea, she made a dash for the door. After practically tumbling out onto the busy high street, she turned her steps downhill. She just hoped that Caroline would be in her office.

Cath hadn't been inside the Crumbleton Times and Echo building before. She knew where it was though, having spotted the little courtyard and the door with the plaque bearing Caroline's name the previous evening when she'd been on a grocery run to Bendall's.

Nerves fluttered in her stomach as she hurtled through the crowds of ambling tourists, doing her best not to turn an ankle on the cobbles or knock anyone over. Cath had a feeling that Caroline Cook was the right person to run her brand new idea past… and with any luck, she'd be the right person to beg for some help too.

Of course, Cath *had* only met her briefly over lunch with Andy. What if she'd just been friendly because of him? What if she didn't want anything to do with her plan?

Cath came to an abrupt halt right beside the steps to the courtyard, almost causing a pile-up as a family carrying an array of fishing nets, shopping bags and super soakers piled straight into her.

'Sorry!' said Cath, grabbing hold of the woman to stop her from falling to the ground as her kids ping-ponged off in different directions, all of them giggling.

The woman shot her an amused look. 'Away with the fairies?'

'Erm… something like that!' muttered Cath. 'Sorry… again.'

'Thanks for the save!' The woman grinned and shrugged before following her family down the hill.

Cath gave herself a little shake. She was being ridiculous. She had no reason to believe that Caroline would be anything other than lovely to her again, and even if she wasn't the right person to help with her grand plan, she'd probably be able to point her in the right direction.

Hurrying up the steps, Cath paused at the door. It was standing wide open, held in place with a metal weight to entice a little bit of fresh air into the building.

Not sure whether she should just wander straight in, Cath knocked anyway.

'Hello? Come on upstairs, I'm in!'

That was definitely Caroline's voice, somewhere from deep within the building. Setting her nerves aside, Cath stepped into the shade of the hallway. As soon as her eyes adjusted to the gloom, she headed up the stairs. There was an office towards the back of the building with its door open, and Cath could see movement inside. It was as good a place to start as any.

'Hi!' said Caroline, beaming at her from behind a huge wooden desk as she approached. She had her bare feet propped up on the top, her toes wriggling as a little fan blew fresh air in a breezy arc. 'Cath, right?'

'Yep!' said Cath, grinning at the pink-faced reporter. 'Sorry to just barge in.'

'Barge away, my friend,' laughed Caroline. 'Anything to distract me from the fact that I'm currently melting. You get bonus points if you've got ice cream.'

'Sorry, no ice cream,' said Cath, sinking into a chair Caroline was waving a hand at. 'I can get you some, though? It's roasting up here!'

'Don't worry,' chuckled Caroline, dropping her feet to the ground and sitting up to face her. 'I was just kidding. I've got to head out in a bit anyway – but I'm loving the impromptu visit. FYI, I'm always happy for a distraction.'

'Good to know,' said Cath, as her nerves melted away.

'So,' said Caroline. 'What can I do you for?'

'I've had an idea... about how to solve the funding issue for the museum,' said Cath.

'You have?' said Caroline, looking intrigued. 'Erm... how long have you been here?'

'Three days,' said Cath.

'And you're not even meant to have started your job yet, am I right?' said Caroline.

'Erm, well... no, but...' Cath's nerves re-emerged in a burst of butterflies. Had she somehow broken an unwritten rule by making a start before she was meant to?

'Don't look so worried!' said Caroline. 'I'm just impressed, that's all.'

'You haven't heard the idea yet,' said Cath with a relieved grin.

'Out with it then!'

'I want to reinstate the Sir Anthony Cheswell tennis tournament as a fundraiser for the museum,' said Cath in a rush.

'Wait,' said Caroline. 'You want to do what?'

Cath took a deep breath and then started to lay the beginnings of her plan out in as much detail as she could.

'So that's it, really,' said Cath, after talking at speed for a full ten minutes without stopping to take a breath. 'I've already unearthed some of the items we'll need, we can do a corresponding display at the museum when we reopen and... well... it's a historic event and the cup's still miraculously in town.'

She paused and looked at Caroline, who didn't say anything.

'I mean, it'll need the dead flies emptying out of it,' she added. 'And a good polish.'

Cath paused again. She knew she needed to stop talking to let Caroline get a word in edgeways... but she was just so desperate for her to *get it* and not dismiss it out of hand. After all, if she had Caroline on her side...

'I love it!' said Caroline with a broad smile.

'You do?' said Cath.

'Of course,' said Caroline. 'It's a brilliant idea. There's plenty of time. We can easily get everything organised in time for next summer and—'

'Next year will be too late!' said Cath, cutting across her. 'From what you said, the museum will probably be boarded up by then. It has to be this year... well... *now*, really. Before the summer's over.'

'Blimey!' said Caroline, sucking air through her teeth. 'You don't mess around, do you?'

Cath shrugged. She wouldn't normally be this forthright, but if it meant the museum had a chance to survive—and she got the chance to stay—well, then a bit of forthrightness would be worth it!

'You know,' said Caroline, after thinking for a moment, 'you might find that Fergus at the hotel would be keen to host the event. Even though it's last minute, we're almost at the end of the summer season, and he's had a bit of a run of bad publicity recently.'

'Uh oh, that doesn't sound so good!' said Cath, as her little bubble of hope deflated slightly. The last thing she needed was to get the museum caught up in any second-hand bad press.

'Nothing major,' said Caroline, waving her hand dismissively. 'Just a matter of someone ending up in hospital after a wedding. It's a bit of a long story, but nothing to do with the food or anything like that—he just got clonked on the head by the bouquet.'

Cath let out a snort of amusement and then clapped her hand over her mouth. 'Sorry,' she muttered. 'Not funny!'

'Oh no, it really was!' said Caroline. 'Anyway, that's how your flat ended up being available... like I said – a very long story, and I'll fill you in over a drink sometime!'

'Sounds like a plan,' said Cath.

'Then you're on,' said Caroline. 'But let's see if we can get this shindig of yours off the ground first. Like I said, Fergus might well be up for something like this—especially if you tell him I'll be covering it in the paper.'

'You will?' said Cath.

'Of course!' said Caroline. 'Now, first things first... you'd better go and find Andy!'

'Okay,' said Cath. 'Erm... why, exactly?'

'Because last time I was at the Dolphin and Anchor, the grass was absolutely wild,' said Caroline. 'He's the one in charge of the mowing, and if he can't get it sorted out in time—or doesn't think it's a possibility for whatever reason—then your idea's sunk.'

'Right,' said Cath, taking a deep breath. Who'd have thought that it would be Andy she was going to have to convince to make it all work?! 'Right. I'll go find him, then. Erm... any ideas where I should start?'

'You know, I think he might be down at the hotel now if you want to catch him,' said Caroline, leaning back in her chair again and popping her feet back on the desk.

'Really?' said Cath.

'Yep,' yawned Caroline. 'I'm sure I heard that ancient mower spluttering earlier.'

'From all the way up here?' said Cath.

'You'd better believe it!'

Cath made a dash for the door and then turned back to smile at Caroline. 'Thank you.'

'Lemme know how it goes!' said Caroline, her eyes drifting closed as the fan swept over her.

CHAPTER 12

ANDY

Andy let out a long breath and wiped the sweat from his forehead with the back of one hand. He was almost finished, and to say he was chuffed with his hard work was the understatement of the century.

The grass had already had three goings over with the mower, and it was looking wonderful—thick and springy, complete with those quintessential stripes. He was going to give it a chance to recover a bit, then he'd give it one more trim with the lowest setting, just to get it looking tennis-court perfect.

After getting Fergus's rather exuberant blessing to tidy up the rest of the garden too, Andy had gone to town with a spot of late summer pruning. The job had ended up being even more rewarding than he'd expected.

The greenery had been harbouring far more of the old wooden signs that Andy had realised. He'd spent some time uncovering them, then he'd braved the bushes and dragged them all out from their hidey-holes and stacked them up against a wall. There was something delightful about the old-fashioned sign writing.

No Drinking On The Court
Please Wear Suitable Shoes
The Umpire's Decision Is Final
Don't Abandon Your Balls In The Bushes

When he was finished with the garden, Andy wanted to give them a fresh lick of paint and a coat of varnish. He had a feeling they'd look fantastic dotted around the edges, somewhere they could be seen properly.

'Right, next!' he said, eyeballing the enormous pile of bush trimmings. He was going to stack them at the back of the compost heap, where they'd make a nice bit of habitat for the town's burgeoning hedgehog population.

Several trips later, the trimmings were gone... and Andy was practically dripping with sweat. It had been hard work getting the garden this far in such a short amount of time, but he had to admit, he'd thoroughly enjoyed himself. He just wanted to go over the grass one more time... but first things first.

Un-popping the front of his overalls, Andy wriggled his arms free. He was far too hot to carry on wearing this many layers. Tying the sleeves around his waist, he revelled in the feel of fresh air on his bare arms. He could really do with a break and a drink in the shade.

'Come on Andy, one more job to do!' he muttered.

It was no good, though. He was still far too hot. Well, there was one easy way he could cool off a bit more while he worked…

Reaching for the hem of his t-shirt, Andy started to yank it up and over his head. It was sticky with sweat, which made the whole process a lot more tricky than it should have been, and he got stuck halfway. After a slightly panicked battle to free himself, he eventually managed to haul it off. Mopping his face with the damp cotton, he was about to toss it aside when Andy noticed he had an audience.

One stunned-looking spectator was staring at him from the entrance to the garden.

'Cath!' he said, feeling his face grow even hotter. 'I'm sorry… I would never have… if I'd known you were there…' he gestured uselessly at his bare chest.

Cath had a peculiar expression on her face that Andy couldn't quite place. Blinking slowly at him, she seemed to be coming out of some kind of daze.

'Hi!' she said, a smile creeping onto her face. It grew wider… and wider. 'Oh my… Andy! You're a genius!'

Andy frowned, not quite sure what was going on… but he didn't get much time to work on the riddle. Cath executed a funny little jump on the spot and then ran towards him. Wrapping her arms around his sweaty neck, she kissed him on the cheek.

Andy promptly lost the power of speech as Cath's flowery scent washed over him. A line of fire spread outwards from the point where her lips had met his face... and the new heat that spread through him had nothing to do with the warmth of the day.

Cath pulled him even closer in the hug, and Andy's arms wrapped around her waist of their own accord as she kissed his cheek again.

'I... erm...' stuttered Andy. 'I'm all sweaty!'

'Okay, so you're a sweaty genius!' laughed Cath, stepping back a little way and grinning up at him.

Andy raised a hand and ruffled his hair, completely confused.

'It's a tennis court!' said Cath, pointing at the newly mown patch of grass.

'Yep, it used to be,' said Andy, not entirely sure why this had just earned him such an enthusiastic greeting. Not that he was complaining, of course! He rather liked getting hugged by Cath... even if he had no idea why he deserved it.

'It's perfect!' said Cath.

'Great!' said Andy. 'Erm... what for?'

'Well, how about we sit over there in the shade,' said Cath, grabbing his hand and tugging. 'I'll fill you in over a drink.'

'I don't think the bar's open,' said Andy faintly, looking at her slender hand wrapped around his big brown one… that he could really do with washing. Hell – he could really do with a shower… maybe a cold one!

'Don't worry!' said Cath, blissfully unaware of the direction his thoughts were wandering in. 'I came prepared.'

Andy followed Cath and watched as she sank down onto a patch of grass in the shade of the newly trimmed bushes.

'I can't believe this,' she said, rummaging in her bag and pulling out two cans of coke.

She handed one to Andy. It was wonderfully cold and judging by the dewy sheen on the outside, it wasn't long out of the fridge.

'Thanks,' he said, cracking it open and taking a grateful slurp of the ice-cold, sugary deliciousness. 'Cheers!' he added, coming up for air long enough to clank his can against the edge of Cath's. 'And… what exactly can't you believe?'

'That great minds think alike on something quite this weird!' chuckled Cath, taking a far more dainty sip of her drink than he just had.

'Okay—I might have had a bit too much sun, but I'm lost,' said Andy.

'The tennis court!' said Cath. 'I was coming to find you to ask if it might be possible to mow it and tidy it up… but you've already done it!'

'Oh,' said Andy. 'Yeah, I have… but… why?'

'It's like this,' said Cath, 'I've had an idea!'

Andy listened as Cath laid out her plans for

reinstating the tennis tournament and raising funds for the museum. In fact... he couldn't take his eyes off her. She seemed to have come alive with excitement—her cheeks were pink and her eyes dancing with life as her words tripped over themselves in her haste to fill him in.

'And I just can't believe you'd had the same idea!' she finished breathlessly.

'Erm... not *quite* the same idea,' hedged Andy, 'but I'm glad it worked out!'

'Glad? I could kiss you!' she beamed at him before taking another swig of coke.

Andy said nothing. Mainly because he'd like nothing more than a kiss from Cath right now... even though he was all sweaty, still shirtless, and in desperate need of a shower.

'Anyway,' said Cath, 'what do you think? Caroline seemed to like the idea, but she wanted me to run it past you. What do you think?' she said again, clearly desperate for his seal of approval.

'I... erm... I think it's a great idea!' said Andy. If he was being honest, he'd have agreed with pretty much anything she said right then, but luckily, he really *did* like the sound of this. 'Anything that brings Crumbleton to life is good in my books. I can have a word with Fergus with you if you'd like?'

'Would you?' she said, her eyes going wide. 'I mean, I really want to do it as soon as we can, while the weather's still good.'

'Of course,' said Andy. 'I think he'll love it. Actually... I'm not sure why no one's ever tried it before. I mean, apart from another cut of the grass and getting the lines painted... and maybe trying to rediscover the terrace... everything here's pretty much good to go. And I could even get the signs finished if you give me a day or two.'

'What signs?' said Cath with interest.

Andy scrambled to his feet and held his hand out to help her up. 'Here, I'll show you.'

'And then we'll go and talk to Fergus?' she said.

'I think I'd better put my tee shirt back on first, don't you?' said Andy with a slightly embarrassed grin.

'Depends,' said Cath, cocking her head and staring at him.

'On what?' said Andy with a surprised laugh.

'On whether the owner of the Dolphin and Anchor is a fan of a very nice view!' she said, flashing him a cheeky grin.

CHAPTER 13

CATH

'Found one!' shouted Cath, yanking the racket out of the crammed box and waving it in the air triumphantly.

It had been a couple of days since she'd had her brainwave about reinstating the Sir Anthony Cheswell Cup, and she'd barely stopped to draw breath since. Still, it would all be worth it. Things were coming together so quickly that she could barely keep up.

As both Caroline and Andy had predicted, Fergus loved the idea. He'd jumped at the chance of hosting an event that could bring a crowd to the hotel—as well as some good publicity. Between them, Cath and Fergus had decided that they'd do their best to keep the event as authentic as possible and include as many nods to the past as they could—it *was* a museum fundraiser, after all.

Fergus's only concern had been about upsetting his

neighbours if tennis balls ended up endangering their windows. Andy had come up with a solution straight away—players could only use old, wooden rackets. They had a lot less power... and in theory, it should make things a little less hairy for everyone involved. The only problem now was finding enough that were in one piece to use on the big day. This was the reason she'd just spent the last two hours with Andy, rummaging through as many boxes at the museum as possible.

'What's that make it?' called Cath over her shoulder. 'Four-two to me?'

'Not that you're competitive or anything?' laughed Andy, peering around a pillar to smile at her.

'Me? Never!' said Cath, before doing a triumphant little fist pump.

'Found one!' yelled Andy.

'Seriously?' said Cath, straightening up and stretching the kinks out of her back.

'Damn,' sighed Andy. 'Strike that, it's a badminton racket.'

Cath let out a snigger.

'Oi, don't mock!' said Andy with an exaggerated pout in her direction.

'As if I would!' said Cath. 'You just look cute when you're sad, that's all.'

The temptation to head straight over there and kiss that pout right off his face was almost more than she could bear... but no, maybe not. The last thing she needed to do right now was scare the living daylights out of the poor guy and send him running for the hills.

Cath was getting more than a little bit used to having Andy around. They'd spent hours on end together over the past few days, getting various things ready for the event... and it was getting... dangerous. She was finding it increasingly hard to stop herself from reaching for him whenever he was nearby. There was something about Andy that made her want to hug him, pat him, brush past him or lean on his shoulder. It was like there was a magnetic charge between them that seemed to be growing stronger by the day. Hell... by the hour!

And yet... maybe she was just imagining it.

Surely not, though?

But maybe.

GAH!

'You okay?' chuckled Andy, staring at her.

'Yeah,' she blurted. 'I mean... yes, why?'

'Because you've gone all frowny,' he said. 'Need a break?'

'You wish!' she said.

No, she didn't need a break... she just needed to get the memory of him topless in the Dolphin and Anchor's garden out of her head. The image was seared into her brain. Not that she was complaining. It just made her a tad... distracted.

As much as she wanted to, Cath definitely wouldn't be rushing over there and snogging his face off. For one thing, if she started, she wasn't sure she'd be able to stop, and for another…

'Hello dearies!'

And for another, there's an elderly lady watching us!

'Hi!' said Cath, plastering a smile onto her face as she turned and hurried towards the new arrival—mainly to stop her from picking her way through the disaster zone. Cath's smile broadened when she spotted what their visitor was carrying.

'I heard you're planning on bringing the Cheswell Cup back to Crumbleton? Said the woman, nodding at her armful of vintage tennis rackets. Some of them were still wearing their wooden cases. 'I had this little lot lying around the house, so I thought I'd pop them up to you in case they might come in handy. I won't need them back… I don't have any use for them anymore.'

'Here, let me take those from you,' said Andy, stepping forward to relieve the woman of her awkward burden.

'What a brilliant donation,' said Cath, doing her best to count the rackets as Andy took them. Their little stash had just doubled in number! 'Can I take your name? I want to make sure everyone who contributes gets a mention in the program—and maybe the newspaper too, if Caroline has got space.'

'Well, wouldn't that be lovely?' said their visitor. 'My name's Evelyn Barker. Good luck with it all, dearie!'

'Wait!' said Cath as Evelyn turned to leave.

The old woman turned to face her again, looking surprised.

'Sorry!' said Cath quickly. 'I just wanted to ask… you're E Barker? *The* E Barker… who won the cup back in 1988?'

'That's me,' said Evelyn.

'Can you tell us anything about the game?' said Cath. 'I mean, I really want to make this year's tournament as authentic as possible, and to share as much of its history as I can, too.'

'I would be delighted to,' said Evelyn. 'I've not had the chance to talk about it all for a good long while… but I'm afraid I'll need to sit down. I'm not as young as I used to be, and the old pins are worn out from climbing the hill carrying that lot!'

'I've got an idea,' said Andy, setting the rackets down carefully. 'How about I treat us all to a cuppa and a cake down at the café?'

'Oh, I don't want to be a bother,' said Evelyn, trying and failing to keep a delighted smile off her face.

'You're a very long way from being a bother,' said Cath, shaking her head. 'And we were just about to take a break anyway.'

'Are you sure?' said Evelyn.

'Positive,' said Andy.

'I might hold you up a bit on the way down the hill,' said Evelyn.

'We're in no rush,' said Andy, 'and you can take my arm if you'd like?'

Cath smiled to herself as Evelyn practically melted on the spot. She wondered briefly if Andy had any idea of the effect he could have by being such a good guy… and then promptly decided that he didn't have a clue. He was just naturally open and friendly. There was no side to him.

Letting out a little sigh, Cath had to shake herself into action.

'Right, sounds like we've got a plan,' she said. 'It'll be nice to get away from all this history for a few minutes!'

∼

Evelyn turned out to be pretty sprightly once she had her hand tucked into the crook of Andy's arm. They were ensconced at one of the café's tables in under ten minutes. After perusing the menu, they ordered a round of toasted teacakes with butter, and a giant pot of tea to share between the three of them.

Cath noticed Evelyn couldn't seem to stop smiling. She kept looking between her and Andy as though she couldn't quite believe her luck. Cath wondered briefly how much company the old woman had at home. It was clear she was having the time of her life with Andy fussing over her.

Yet again, Cath felt a rush of tingles as the

beginnings of another idea started to bloom in the back of her mind. She wanted the museum to be at the heart of the community… maybe people like Evelyn were the key to making that happen.

Cath bit her lip. She needed to keep this brand-new idea to herself for the time being and think it through properly in the peace and quiet of her flat. Right now, she wanted to hear all about the last bout of the Cheswell Cup from the reigning champion herself.

'So, tell us all about it!' she said, smiling across the table at Evelyn. 'I've seen photos of some of the earlier tournaments, but there weren't many from the eighties —at least, not in the only album I've found so far.'

'I might have some more photos at home,' said Evelyn. 'If you'd like to see them, I could look them out?'

'That would be brilliant!' said Cath.

'But tell us, what was it like,' said Andy. 'How were the games organised… or was it a bit of a free-for-all? There's only one court, after all.'

'Oh no,' said Evelyn. 'It was very well organised. It was open to all comers—male and female. I remember I had to work my way through a bunch of preliminaries, then there were the semis, and eventually, I was up against Nigel Finlay-Warren in the final. And I won!'

'You make it sound so easy,' chuckled Andy.

'Not that last match,' said Evelyn, her eyes going dreamy. 'I do remember that Nigel wasn't very happy about it though. He almost beat me and I had to survive several match points. He had this fantastic serve, you see—but I worked him out eventually, and beat him in the final set.'

'Wow,' said Cath. 'Sounds like quite a game!'

'It was brilliant fun, but of course, the tennis club closed its doors not long after that. Before we knew it, Fergus had bought the building and turned it into a hotel—and now we've got the Dolphin and Anchor.' Evelyn paused and smiled at both of them in turn. 'Nothing stays the same, of course—and I like Fergus's cooking very much—but I'm glad you're bringing back the Cheswell Cup. I'll definitely be coming along to watch.'

At that moment, a smiling woman bearing a tray laden with teacakes and a teapot rocked up at the table.

'Ah, Mabel!' said Evelyn with a broad smile. 'You angel.'

'I don't know about that,' chuckled Mabel, efficiently emptying her tray onto the table.

'I didn't get to introduce you the other day when we were in with Caroline,' said Andy. 'Mabel, this is Cath—she's taking on the museum.'

'Oof! You're a brave soul!' said Mabel, beaming at her.

'And she's starting out by bringing tennis back to town,' said Evelyn.

'The Cheswell Cup?' said Mabel in surprise.

'The very one,' said Cath. 'Fergus down at the

Dolphin and Anchor has already agreed, so it's all systems go.'

'Well well well!' said Mabel. 'I remember the last one when our Evelyn here won. Of course, I was just a tiny tacker back then. I spent most of the day with Geraldine from the antiques shop, pilfering bowls of strawberries and hiding under the tablecloths to eat them.'

Cath smiled. 'Strawberries seem to have been a major part of the proceedings—they even featured heavily in the photo album I found.'

'Oh yes, you can't hold the Cheswell Cup without plenty of strawberries,' said Evelyn, taking a hearty bite of buttery teacake.

'Sounds like we know what our next job is going to be, then!' said Cath raising her eyebrows at Andy.

He nodded. 'I'm sure we'll be able to sort something out.'

'Talk to Stuart down at Bendall's,' said Mabel. 'I'll bet my bottom dollar he'll be able to point you in the right direction.'

CHAPTER 14

ANDY

'Hello? Cath, you in here?'

Andy came to a halt at the makeshift barrier Cath had constructed out of several panels of loaned puppy fencing. After Evelyn's surprise visit, they'd decided they needed to do something to ensure visitors didn't wander into the disaster zone in search of Cath and risk getting crushed by the teetering piles of rubbish.

Considering he'd helped Cath to shift an entire van full of recycling out of the building the previous day, Andy couldn't quite fathom how it somehow felt *more* cramped in here than before.

'I'm here! Two secs, I'll come to you!'

Cath's voice reached him from somewhere near the back wall, but for the life of him, he couldn't see her, no matter how much he craned his neck.

'EEP!'

Crash!

The surprised squeak had been closely followed by a cave-in of what looked like an eight-foot-high stack of old newspapers.

'Do I need to send in a rescue party?!' he called.

'I'm good! Save yourself!'

Cath's laughing face appeared at last, and Andy felt the now-familiar flip in his stomach at the sight of her. How *anyone* could be quite so bouncy and enthusiastic while surrounded by so much rubbish was beyond him. But Cath's enthusiasm was infectious… and from what he'd witnessed over the past few days, it wasn't just him that was falling a little bit in love with their new curator.

It had turned out that reinstating the Cheswell Cup had been the perfect opportunity for Cath to meet a whole load of Crumbleton's residents in a seriously short amount of time. Caroline had popped a call-to-action on the newspaper's social media pages, asking anyone with memories, photos, or memorabilia of the competition to contact Cath at the museum. The news had spread like wildfire, and there had been a steady trickle of visitors turning up ever since.

'Have a seat!' yelled Cath. 'I need to clear a path to you. It'll take me a moment!'

Andy grinned and flopped down into the old sofa that was now in pride of place on one side of the little hallway. He'd given Cath a hand to deep-clean it, and now it was coming into its own as part of the makeshift visitors' centre. The hallway was the only clear, clean and safe spot in the whole museum, and Cath had needed somewhere to sit with the visitors and take notes as they told her their stories... preferably without having to risk their necks in the process.

'Okay, I'm here!' puffed Cath, shifting the fence a little so that she could sidle around it. 'Sorry about that, I was just trying to disentangle the net a bit and I got the corner caught on a pile of newspapers.'

'Ah... that explains the landslide,' said Andy, turning to smile at her as she collapsed into the sofa next to him with a happy sigh.

'Yep, but it's fine... they were destined for the next recycling run anyway, so no harm done really.'

'Blimey,' said Andy, raising an eyebrow. 'That's very decisive of you!'

Cath had been cautious about getting rid of any of the thousands of newspapers they'd unearthed, just in case they held a record of "something important" within their pages. So the news that she was ready to discard an eight-foot stack of history was rather surprising.

'It was an easy decision,' said Cath, returning his smile. 'The whole stack was made up of hundreds of copies of the same issue of the Crumbleton Times and Echo from the 1990s. I figure I only need to keep one of them to check there's nothing important in there!'

'Or Caroline might know something about it,' said Andy.

'Good call, I'll ask her… just in case,' said Cath. 'In a way, I hope I can just scrap them all with a clear conscience—I swear it's getting worse back there, not better!'

'Yeah… I thought that too,' said Andy. 'Is it me, or is there more stuff in here than when I stopped by to pick up the line-painting machine yesterday?'

'Yep!' said Cath, rolling her eyes. 'Caroline's post on social media has been brilliant for gathering a bit of social history—and meeting half the town all in one go—but the drawback is they all turn up with stuff they want to donate.'

'You can start saying "no" you know,' chuckled Andy.

'I have,' said Cath. 'Just this morning, I sent Stuart Bendall's elderly mum away with a bunch of "vintage" plastic jelly moulds she wanted to donate.'

'You did what?' gasped Andy in mock outrage. 'But… you might need them!'

'I might?' said Cath, looking concerned.

'Think of the history! I can't believe you'd just cast it aside like that!' Andy elbowed her gently in the ribs.

'Git!' she chuckled, nudging him right back. 'You'll be glad to know I did keep one of her donations though. A really important one.'

'Oh?' said Andy, doing his best not to get lost in the tiny navy flecks dancing in Cath's eyes.

'Here,' she said. Leaning forward, she grabbed a tin from the top of an upturned tea chest acting as a makeshift coffee table. Cath prised the lid off and wafted the contents under his nose.

'Shortbread?' he said.

'Only the best shortbread I've ever tasted,' she said, taking a piece and gesturing for him to do the same. 'Even better, Agatha's volunteered to bake a whole ton of it for the tournament. Apparently, the WI ladies are keen to help too, and they want to know if Fergus would be willing for them to run a cake stall on the day —all proceeds going to the museum.'

'That's brilliant!' said Andy, taking a bite and then letting out a whimper of delight as the buttery sweetness dissolved on his tongue. 'Oh. My. Goodness.'

'Right?' said Cath.

Andy nodded, taking another bite.

'Oh,' she said, 'and Agatha mentioned they'd be happy to be in charge of doling out the strawberries and cream too.'

'Ah,' said Andy, 'so... that's actually what I came to talk to you about. Stuart can't get the strawberries.'

'But... I thought Stuart could basically get anything?' Cath frowned. 'I mean his shop is...'

'A modern miracle?' said Andy, nodding. There couldn't be that many places in the world where you could grab a pint of milk and a set of chimney-sweeping brushes at the same time.

'He really can't get us the strawberries?' said Cath. 'I

don't mean to sound like a drama lama, but that could be a bit of a disaster. I mean, literally every single person I've had in here has asked whether there'll be local strawberries.'

'Yeah,' sighed Andy. 'He was really sorry. It's quite late in the season as it is, and it's got something to do with the bad weather at the start of the summer wiping out most of his supplier's crop. The other guy he thought might be able to help has just retired.'

'Gutted,' said Cath.

'He said he could get his hands on plenty of blueberries… or gooseberries… or rhubarb…' Andy trailed off. It was pretty clear from the look on her face what Cath thought of those options.

'Okay, well… don't get your hopes up, but I do have another idea.'

'Tell me!' said Cath, immediately perking up.

'Well, there's this garden I can see into when I mend the town steps,' said Andy. 'It belongs to old Harold Pottinger, and I know I've seen strawberries growing in there before. I'm not sure how many, mind, but it might be worth asking?'

'Is it a big garden?' said Cath. 'I mean, we're going to need quite a lot.'

'Not sure,' said Andy. 'His wife makes jam I think, so there's a good chance he grows a decent crop.'

'But surely they'll be spoken for?' said Cath.

Andy shrugged. 'Shall we go and find out?'

'Why not?' Cath nodded, jumping to her feet. 'I could do with a break from the boxes anyway.'

∽

Andy couldn't help but send up his silent thanks for the narrow steps as Cath trotted down the hill ahead of him. If they had been able to walk side-by-side, it would have been as much as he could do not to reach out and take her hand. He hadn't wanted to let go when she'd pulled him up out of the sofa just now, and he could swear his palms were still tingling from contact.

Idiot!

They might be spending lots of time together, but Andy wasn't about to kid himself. Although Cath seemed to be happy whenever he was around, he knew she was probably just being polite. He knew she was glad of his help, but he was under no allusions—Cath Walker was about as capable as they came. She could do all this on her own... blindfolded.

Still, Andy liked helping her and it was the perfect excuse to spend more time with her. What he'd do after the weekend, when the Cheswell Cup was awarded and the tournament was all over... well he didn't want to think about that right now.

'How far down is it?' said Cath, pausing about five steps below and peering back at him over her shoulder.

'See that white house there?' he said, pointing at the

upper floors of a classic Crumbleton townhouse above the stone walls and greenery.

Cath nodded. 'And we can really see into their garden from back here?'

'Just a tiny part, but yes,' said Andy, hurrying after her and then pointing at a gap where the high stone wall met a patch of laurel hedge.

Cath leaned in, using her hands to part the glossy leaves so that she could peer through.

'I see strawberries!' she said excitedly.

'Great!' said Andy with a sigh of relief. Just because he'd seen them there in previous years didn't mean Harold was necessarily growing them again this year. That's why they'd decided to check it out first. 'Come on, let's go knock on the door and find out more.'

The pair of them cut through a side alley back onto the high street, emerging just across the road from the Crumbleton Times and Echo offices.

Andy led the way past a couple of buildings up the hill and then knocked on a smart, navy blue front door.

'Andy?'

Andy beamed at the elderly gent who'd just opened the door. His white candyfloss hair fluttered slightly in the breeze, and he leaned heavily on a wooden walking stick.

'Hi Harold. Sorry to drop in unannounced,' said Andy.

'Don't apologise, dear boy,' said Harold with a broad smile. 'I like company, and unexpected company is even better... especially when they turn up with beautiful women in tow!'

Andy grinned as a splutter of surprised laughter escaped from Cath.

'Harold, let me introduce Cath Walker, she's—'

'Ah!' said Harold, cutting across him. 'Our new curator. Yes... the town's abuzz with your exploits!'

'It is?' said Cath in surprise.

'Certainly,' said Harold, nodding and looking impressed. 'Here not much more than a week, and you're already making the headlines.'

'I've got Caroline to thank for that,' said Cath, smiling at him.

'Hmm, more like your own hard work, I suspect,' said Harold.

Andy nodded in agreement.

'Well, I was hoping you might come to see me,' he added, before beckoning them both to follow him inside.

Cath raised her eyebrows at Andy briefly, but he just grinned at her and stood back so that she could follow on behind Harold. After all, he was just there to make the introductions. Cath was the one with the magic touch when it came to making the whole of Crumbleton fall in love with her.

'Erm... wow!' breathed Cath, as they followed Harold along a narrow hallway and into a large kitchen at the back of the building.

Andy knew she wasn't talking about the house itself

—as lovely as it was. He had a feeling her surprise might be more down to the fact that every available nook and cranny was stuffed with jars of jam. No matter which way he looked, pretty, cloth-frilled jars with gleaming, ruby-red conserve stared back at him.

'That's a lot, Harold!' chuckled Andy.

'The jam?' said the old man, sinking into a chair at the scrubbed kitchen table and indicating for them to do the same.

Andy nodded and watched as Cath inspected some of the handwritten labels on the jars lining the old-fashioned wooden dresser.

'It's the wife,' said Harold. 'She's obsessed. She's out at the moment, otherwise I'd introduce you. She'll be back soon enough, though.'

'But... this is several years' worth!' gasped Cath, staring around at the hundreds of jars.

'You don't need to tell me that, love,' said Harold. 'More than I can eat in several lifetimes. We've been together for more than fifty years... and she's made strawberry jam every single one of them.'

'Wow,' breathed Andy.

'Wow doesn't cover it, lad,' said Harold with a smile. 'I don't have the heart to tell her I prefer marmalade!'

Cath snorted and her laugh was echoed by Harold.

'Sorry,' she muttered.

'You young people apologise too much!' he said in amusement. 'Anyway, I'm guessing you've come to see me about my strawberries?'

'We have!' said Andy in surprise. 'But how did you...?'

'I had a feeling you might be after some the minute I heard you were bringing back the Cheswell Cup,' he said. 'Good news for you is—being this side of the hill —mine are always on the late side to ripen up. So I've not picked the blighters yet.'

'And you'd be willing for us to have them for the event?' said Andy.

'Willing? You'd be doing me a favour,' said Harold with a decided nod. 'Annie's already started to mither about me picking them at the weekend so that she can make this year's jam... but there's no way she'd deprive a good cause! They can be my donation... and you might just be saving the house from a giant jam explosion.'

'Wow, thank you,' said Cath, coming to sit next to Andy.

He could feel the warmth and excitement coming off her in waves. He only hoped she wasn't getting her hopes up for nothing. They might have seen a few plants through the gap in the hedge, but the fruit they'd seen would barely be enough to feed the pair of them, let alone half the town.

'Erm... do you think there might be enough for several portions?' said Andy, not quite sure how to ask the question without offending the elderly gent.

'Enough?' hooted Harold. 'Why don't you come outside and see for yourselves?'

CHAPTER 15

CATH

'So, how's it all going? Feeling ready?' asked Caroline from the depths of Cath's patchwork sofa.

Cath grinned at her as she poured a generous glass of red wine for them both. 'Define ready...'

'Everything in place. No imminent disasters. World domination ensured,' said Caroline accepting her glass with a nod of thanks as Cath sank down next to her.

'Well then... I think I'm royally feckered!' said Cath, raising her glass in a mock toast.

Caroline snorted. 'Excellent. Loving that confidence. Seriously, though?'

'Seriously, I think everything is as in place as it can be,' said Cath. 'It's way too late to sell tickets or anything like that, so there's no way of knowing how many people are going to turn up... or if *anyone's* going to turn up, for that matter.'

'Don't worry, they'll come,' said Caroline.

'I hope so,' said Cath, feeling the now familiar flutter of nerves as she just about managed to hold off crossing her fingers around the stem of her glass. 'Anyway, if they do, we'll be ready for them. We've got plenty of wooden rackets now, thanks to Evelyn Barker's donation.'

Caroline nodded and scribbled Evelyn's name down in her notebook next to the word "rackets". 'Who else goes on the list?'

This was the real reason Caroline was in Cath's flat, after all. She was there on official newspaper business, collecting the names of everyone who was pitching in to make the event a success. Of course, the fact that the *official business* happened to coincide with Cath's invitation to drink wine and eat cheese made the whole thing far more fun.

'The WI are running a cake stall and providing jugs of Pimms and mocktails—with Fergus's blessing of course. Obviously, I want to thank Fergus and the staff at the Hotel. Then there's Stuart at Bendall's—he's donated the cream to go with the strawberries, and Milly at the flower shop is making little posies as gifts for the winner of each round. She's donating a big bunch as a raffle prize too. Actually, I'll just give you a copy of the list of the prizes and everyone who's donated, because it's about a mile long.'

Caroline nodded, still scribbling hard and Cath paused to let her catch up.

'Anyone else?' said Caroline. 'I mean, I'll make more notes tomorrow, but I don't want to miss anyone.'

'Annie Pottinger is doing a jam sale to raise money, Harold is donating the strawberries, and I guess I'd better thank the council for lending us the deckchairs from Crumbleton Sands.'

'Those lovely stripey vintage ones?' said Caroline.

'Yep. Andy's already brought them over. Actually—make sure Andy gets name-checked—right at the top if you don't mind! He's been brilliant, the guy's hardly stopped. He's done all the work on the court, and I've roped him in to help me pick the strawberries from Harold's tomorrow morning so that they're as fresh as they can be for when we kick things off at eleven.'

'That boy's being *very* helpful these days,' said Caroline, wriggling her eyebrows.

'I'd hardly call Andy a boy,' said Cath with a straight face, deliberately ignoring the less-than-subtle undertones to Caroline's pronouncement.

'Okay, fine,' said Caroline. 'Lemme ask this, then—is Andy your *manfriend?*'

Cath snorted with laughter, almost inhaling a mouthful of wine. She couldn't help it. There was something about Caroline that made keeping a straight face pretty much impossible.

'I couldn't possibly comment,' spluttered Cath.

'Blimey, you picked that up fast,' grumbled Caroline.

'Picked what up fast?' said Cath, suddenly lost.

'The *no-comment* thing,' she huffed. 'One of the drawbacks of being the town's only reporter Is that I get "no comment" from all my friends whenever I want to engage in a bit of harmless gossip!'

'Aw,' said Cath. 'Sad for you, but still… no comment.'

'Spoilsport,' said Caroline with a pout. 'For what it's worth, I think the pair of you would make a very cute couple.'

'Well… I…' Cath took a deep breath, wondering when the little flat had grown quite so warm. 'Here's the thing, I'm not sure I want to be half of a cute couple just yet. Not considering it's taken a couple of particularly tricky years to forget about the gittish other half of the last cute couple I was part of.'

'Oh,' said Caroline. 'Poo. Sorry.'

Cath shrugged. 'That's life, right?'

'It doesn't have to be like that,' said Caroline, shaking her head. 'Not all blokes are first-class asshats.'

'Is your bloke one of the exceptions?' said Cath.

'I don't have one,' said Caroline. 'Mainly because the ones who *aren't* first-class asshats are either taken or I've known them since we were wearing identical baby rompers and sharing toddler paddling pools.'

'Cute!' chuckled Cath.

'Erm, nope. Far far far too close for comfort. For example—your Andy? Kissing him would be like snogging my brother.'

'Eww!'

'Yes,' agreed Caroline. 'Maximum ick factor right there, my friend.'

'Okay I get it,' said Cath. 'But still… I'm not sure I'm ready.'

'But if you were?' said Caroline.

'If I was… he's seriously cute,' said Cath, keeping her eyes on her glass of wine. 'Especially without a top on.'

'Cath Walker, you naughty girl!' squeaked Caroline. 'And also, EWW!'

Cath grinned at her. 'I do like him. He's been lovely to me. But… I've only been in town for five minutes.'

'Yep, and in that time you seem to have managed to charm half of Crumbleton's population,' said Caroline.

'I don't know about that,' said Cath awkwardly.

'Well I do—it's kind of my job, after all!' said Caroline. 'Enough people have stopped me in the street to tell me they think you're the best thing to arrive in town since Ruby Hutchinson – and she's a bloomin' celebrity author!'

'Well, thanks,' said Cath, taking a fortifying sip of her wine. 'I mean, I'm flattered, but—'

'You know what else they've all been telling me?' said Caroline with a decidedly naughty smile.

'What?' said Cath.

'That they haven't seen our Andy look this happy in years.'

'Oh,' said Cath.

'Exactly.'

'Erm... I'm not saying I *am* going to do anything about it,' said Cath, 'but... if I was... is there, I mean... has there been... I mean...'

'You want to know about his current relationship status?' said Caroline.

'I... maybe?' said Cath.

Caroline rolled her eyes. 'He's single.'

'I guessed that bit,' said Cath, doing her best not to let her frustration show in her voice. 'The real question is... why?'

'That's easy,' said Caroline. 'You're not going to find any skeletons in that closet. The man is exactly as he appears. Sweet, friendly, lovely, straightforward.'

'So... he's just... single?' said Cath. 'How?'

'Because his bitch of an ex-girlfriend was a screwed-up mess,' huffed Caroline. 'I'm sure Tara was a perfectly nice person... *deep* down. But she seemed to crave drama. It was like she was always spoiling for a fight. She picked at everything—anything Andy did was wrong. His job was wrong. His clothes were wrong. His smile was wrong.'

'That sounds horrible,' said Cath with a frown.

'She wanted to change him,' said Caroline.

'Why would *anyone* want Andy to change?' said Cath, almost to herself. The man was practically perfect.

Caroline was smirking again, and Cath wondered for a moment if that last thought had managed to escape out of her mouth.

'What happened with them?' said Cath quickly. 'In the end, I mean.'

'She issued an ultimatum,' said Caroline. 'She wanted to move away from Crumbleton—up to London—and if Andy wanted to save the relationship, he'd have to move too.'

'And he didn't,' said Cath.

'Nope, he didn't,' said Caroline. 'That man's first and true love will always be Crumbleton. Hell, he single-handedly keeps the old place from crumbling, if you'll excuse the pun. I don't think he'll ever leave, and any potential love interests will just have to resign themselves to the fact that they're going to be entering into an Andy-Crumbleton threesome situation.'

Cath let out a surprised laugh, almost spraying Caroline with wine.

'Sorry!' she gasped.

'I don't know what you're laughing about, young lady!' said Caroline, raising an eyebrow. 'It's you who's going to have to deal with this particular menage!'

'Only if I'm in a relationship with him,' said Cath, shifting uncomfortably. 'Which I'm not.'

'Yet,' added Caroline. 'But let's just say it went that way... hypothetically... how would you feel about the whole Crumbleton thing?'

'Well, I've not been here long,' said Cath slowly, 'but let's just say I can see where he's coming from. I'm already starting to feel the same about the place. Give me a couple more weeks and I can imagine I'll never want to leave.'

Caroline grinned at her. 'Then we'd better make sure tomorrow's fundraiser goes with a bang.'

~

'I can't believe the big day's here already!' said Andy, as the pair of them headed down the high street towards Harold and Annie's townhouse.

Andy was carrying a stack of sturdy, shallow cardboard boxes Stuart from Bendall's had given them. They were perfect for picking the strawberries and ferrying them safely down to the Dolphin and Anchor.

'I know,' yawned Cath, wishing she had time to nip into the café and beg Mabel for a large cup of Earl Grey to keep her going. 'I didn't sleep a wink last night!'

'I'm not surprised,' said Andy. 'You've been working too hard.'

'Erm… no, that'd be you!' laughed Cath. 'I've just been along for the ride.'

'That's rubbish and you know it,' said Andy.

'Fine. But it's been fun, not work. And… thank you, by the way.' Cath swallowed. She was suddenly feeling weirdly emotional as well as completely knackered. 'I couldn't have done this without you.'

'Yes you could,' said Andy, sounding matter of fact. 'I've got a feeling you could do pretty much anything once you've set your mind to it.'

'Are you saying I'm stubborn?' said Cath, shooting a sideways grin at him. It was far easier to make a joke than take the compliment.

'No—just one of the most capable people I've ever come across,' he said. 'And by the way, that's basically the highest compliment I can come up with.'

'Well… thanks,' said Cath, coming to a halt next to him in front of the Pottingers' front door.

'You're welcome,' he said.

'And… just for the record,' said Cath as Andy knocked on the door, 'even if I *could* have done it without you, I wouldn't have wanted to.'

Cath watched as Andy's entire face creased into a delighted smile, and it felt like the sun had just come up.

'Well well well,' said Annie Pottinger, as she threw the door open and beamed out at them, 'if it isn't Crumbleton's new lovebirds!'

'I…' said Andy.

'We…' started Cath, feeling like she'd just been winded.

'There isn't…' said Andy.

'We're not together,' said Cath. She instantly wanted

to kick herself—she could swear Andy had just winced when she'd said that!

'No,' he said quietly, 'we're not. Just friends... here for the strawberries.'

'Hmm,' muttered Annie. 'We'll see about that. Come on in then, those strawberries aren't going to pick themselves!'

CHAPTER 16

ANDY

Andy trailed after the two women, glad that he was carrying the stack of cardboard boxes. They gave him something to hide his face behind. Not that he really needed to—Cath didn't glance back at him once as they followed Annie down the hallway and through to the kitchen. He wondered if she was feeling as discombobulated as he was from Annie's good-natured prodding.

Swallowing hard, Andy gave his head a little shake, trying to get his thoughts back in order. Today wasn't the day for exploring what was—or *wasn't*—there between them. Nor was it the day for awkward silences and longing glances. Cath had worked so hard to pull this event together in such a short amount of time, and there was no way a bit of good-natured town gossip was going to throw a spanner in the works... at least, not if he had anything to do with it!

'Ah! The strawberry pickers!' cheered Harold from his perch at the kitchen table.

Andy smiled at him over the boxes. 'Present and correct.'

'Wow, it looks different in here!' said Cath staring around the kitchen.

Andy knew what she meant... something had definitely changed since their last visit. He just couldn't put his finger on what.

'No jam on show,' said Annie, somewhat morosely. 'We brought the car up last night while the high street was quiet and loaded it all up, ready to bring down to the Dolphin and Anchor for today's stall.'

Andy nodded. Yep, that would explain it. There were several hundred jars missing and all the nooks and crannies were empty. The old dresser looked practically naked without them.

'Thank you so much,' said Cath. 'It's incredibly generous of you.'

'Better that it all gets eaten,' said Annie. 'Besides, it gives me plenty of space to make some new batches.'

Andy had to bite the inside of his cheek to stop a hoot of laughter from escaping at the look of horror that had just crossed Harold's face.

'On that note,' said Cath, 'are you *really* sure you don't mind us picking all your strawberries?'

'We're sure!' said Harold quickly, widening his eyes as the horror in them intensified. He glanced down at the toast in front of him—smothered in strawberry jam—then back up to Cath with an air of pleading.

Andy snorted and quickly tried to pass it off as a sneeze.

'Why?' said Annie. 'Don't you need them? Because—'

'We definitely need them!' said Andy quickly, earning himself a grateful wink from Harold.

'Well then, we don't mind,' said Annie. 'We can't let the town down at the last minute. Harold will just have to make do with something different on his toast.'

'Maybe... some marmalade?' said Harold hopefully.

It was Cath's turn to bite her lip. She was clearly struggling to keep a straight face as much as he was.

'If that's what you'd like, my love, I'll give it a go,' said Annie, beaming at her husband, who looked like he was about to go into shock.

'Shall we make a start?' Andy said quietly to Cath.

There was something about the palpable devotion in the air that was making him feel weirdly emotional. He needed to get back outside in the fresh air and gather his wits.

'Good idea,' said Cath. 'It's going to take Fergus's team ages to get them all washed and prepared... so we'd better get going!'

'Start up at the top terrace,' said Harold, 'and work your way down. That way, by the time your back's killing you from bending over, you won't still be trekking all the way up the steps to the top.'

'Roger that,' said Andy, nodding his thanks.

'I'll grab the door!' said Cath, dashing over to slide open the heavy French windows.

Andy waited for her to lead the way and then followed with the stack of boxes. He paused just outside to take a deep breath of fresh air.

'You okay?' said Cath, raising a quizzical eyebrow at him.

Andy nodded. 'Just thinking what a perfect day it is for the event.'

It might have been a hastily concocted cover story for the fact that he was staring blankly up at the sky, but it was at least true. The high, scattered clouds were drifting lazily against a robin-egg sky. The breeze was light and fresh—perfect for staying cool without being enough to wreak havoc on any of the stalls.

Andy stooped to pop the stack of boxes down on the ground. 'I vote we take one each, fill it, and then pile them up here as we go?'

'Sounds like a plan,' said Cath, grabbing one. 'Race you!'

Andy smiled as she pelted off up the steep steps towards the top terrace. He blew out a sigh of relief as her playful attitude promptly melted the lingering awkwardness that had been threatening to body-snatched him.

Following at a slightly more leisurely pace, Andy admired the different levels of the garden as he climbed the steep steps. There were five levels in all, and other than a couple of brightly-coloured flower beds on the first terrace, the entire lot was set to strawberry plants, and all of them were dripping with fruit.

Considering how steep the garden was, it was a bit of a miracle that Harold managed to navigate it with his stick. It was evident that he spent a lot of time out there, though. Andy didn't think he'd ever come across such pampered plants before. Their deep green leaves rested on a nest of golden straw—clearly there to keep the large, glossy berries out of the dirt and as far away from any rampaging slugs as possible.

'They look a bit like jewels, don't they?' said Cath as he joined her on the top terrace.

'I was just thinking that,' said Andy. 'Right... let's see who can fill a box the fastest!'

The pair of them worked together in companionable silence, and by the time their boxes were full to overflowing, they seemed to have barely made a dent in what was on offer.

'I'm glad we started early,' said Cath, as they both carried their full loads down to the bottom, only to switch them out for empty boxes. 'We could be here all day at this rate...'

'We've got plenty of time, don't worry,' said Andy, shooting her a smile. 'Besides, we'll run out of boxes before then.'

'Good point,' said Cath with a grin. 'In that case... I'm taking two up with me!'

By the time they'd cleared the top two terraces of juicy berries, Andy knew what Harold had been talking about when he'd mentioned a sore back. His thighs were burning from bending over so much too, and he was parched.

'You know,' said Cath, hefting her full boxes carefully into her arms, 'I got a feeling I'm going to smell of strawberries for all eternity after this.'

'I can think of worse things to smell of,' said Andy, straightening up slowly and doing his best not to let out a weary groan.

'I wonder if they taste as good as they smell,' said Cath.

'You're kidding me!' said Andy. 'You're not telling me you haven't tried one yet?'

Cath shook her head. 'Why—have you?'

'Two for the box, one for Andy… two for the box… two for Andy!' he laughed.

'You gannet!' chuckled Cath.

'You're missing out,' said Andy. 'Try one!'

'I've kind of got my hands full here,' said Cath.

Without thinking, Andy plucked the fattest, juiciest strawberry out of the boxes in her arms and held it up for her.

Cath stared at it for a long moment, then her eyes flicked to him, and then back to the strawberry. Just as Andy realised what a decidedly intimate position he'd managed to land them in, Cath ducked her head and took a bite.

'Good?' said Andy, his voice slightly hoarse.

'Mmm!' she mumbled, chewing with a huge grin on her face.

Andy swallowed. There was a trail of dark red juice making its way down her chin.

'You've got…' he said, reaching out and wiping the juice away with his thumb.

Cath's eyes widened and locked with his.

'Sorry,' he gasped. 'I didn't… I…'

But Cath was leaning in. He could see those dancing flecks of navy blue in her eyes…

'Ah ha! I knew it!'

Startled, both Andy and Cath spun around—several strawberries scattering from the top of Cath's box in the process. There, staring at them with an avid look on her face, was Annie Pottinger. She had a tea tray in her hands bearing two steaming mugs of tea and a plate of strawberry jam sandwiches.

'Don't mind me,' she grinned, popping the tray down onto the grass. 'I'll leave you two to it.'

'I…' said Cath.

'We…' said Andy.

It was too late, Annie was already trotting away down the steps.

Cath cast an awkward glance at him, looking decidedly pink in the face.

'Let's get this job finished,' she muttered.

'How's it going, Andy mate?'

'Brilliant!' said Andy, grinning up from his spot behind the entrance table to find Oli from the bookshop smiling at him.

'Blimey—it's heaving back here!' he laughed. 'How much to get in?'

Andy pointed at the laminated list of modest entrance fees. There was one rate for spectators and a slightly higher one for players.

'I'm watching and Ruby's playing,' said Oli, grabbing his wallet from his pocket and handing over a twenty-pound-note. 'She'll be down in a sec, she's just getting changed.'

'Fab!' said Andy. 'Two secs, I'll grab you some change.'

'Keep it as a donation,' said Oli, shaking his head.

'Cheers!' said Andy, adding it to the pot. It had been happening so often that he was no longer surprised by the generosity—though he was just as grateful as the first time. Crumbleton was showing its true colours today. He had a feeling they'd probably already exceeded any fundraising target Cath might have had in mind... and they were only about an hour into proceedings!'

'And... is there a raffle table? Someone said...'

'In the tent over there,' said Andy, pointing towards the marquee Cath had borrowed from a nearby cricket club. 'The WI ladies are looking after it. There's also an amazing display on the history of the tournament.

There are some great photos, and the old line-painting machine's in there too! And bonus—there's tea and cake, mocktails, Pimms, strawberries and cream...'

'Heaven!' laughed Oli. 'I'll head over there now. I've got an early hardback copy of Ruby's next book here to add to the raffle prizes. I got her to sign it.'

'I'll be sure to tell Cath,' said Andy, waving Oli off as he made his way towards the marquee, only to be pounced on by the gaggle of WI ladies the minute he wandered inside.

Andy grinned and settled back into his deckchair. He'd angled it so that he could half-watch the players when he wasn't busy having cash thrown at him left right and centre.

'Is the *Match Maker* back?'

Andy sat up again, only to find Kendra—one of the young waitresses from the hotel—dancing from foot to foot in front of his table. She was wearing tennis whites, and clearly waiting for her turn on the court.

'Sorry,' he laughed, 'Lee's got it. See if you can grab it from him when he comes off?'

'Cool, thanks Andy, I will,' said Kendra, jogging off.

Andy chuckled. The old wooden rackets had proved to be a huge hit—not least because some were brilliant, and some... not so much. Even though he and Cath had given them a once-over to check they were safe, they'd not managed to catch all the issues. Some of them had slightly saggy strings, and others had patches of woodworm they'd completely failed to spot. This had caused a great deal of hilarity when the racket Caroline chose for her preliminary match simply broke in half on her first serve.

The *Match Maker*—as it had been dubbed—had quickly become the racket of choice. It had decent strings and, so far, it hadn't disintegrated on anyone mid-game.

'Andy love?'

Andy sat up again. He'd just been distracted by the sight of Cath walking hand-in-hand with a little girl who was busy chattering nineteen to the dozen. He'd barely had the chance to speak to her since they'd arrived… but there would be plenty of time for that later. This was her big day, and she seemed to be in her element—dashing around, making sure everyone had drinks and cake, strawberries and tennis rackets. He couldn't be more proud of her.

'Yoo-hoo? Earth to Andy?'

'Sorry Mabel, sorry!' he laughed, turning to face her.

'No worries, love,' she said, popping a tray down onto the table next to him.

'What's all this?' he said.

'Cath just nipped into the tent and asked us if we could bring some lunch over to you,' said Mabel. 'She didn't want you to miss out just because you're stuck over here.'

'I'm not missing out,' said Andy. 'I'm having the best time.'

'That's because you're a sweetheart,' said Mabel, reaching over and patting him on the cheek. 'We all think that… and Cath does too.'

'I… erm… we're just friends!' said Andy.

'We'll see,' chuckled Mabel, wandering back towards the tent and the rest of the WI ladies.

'Oh lord,' sighed Andy, noticing that they were all waiting for her at the entrance, with identical, keen looks on their faces. It looked like he and Cath were the talk of the town, whether it was warranted or not.

Andy glanced down at the tray and smiled. The delivery might have been a tad embarrassing, but he could hug Cath for thinking of him. There was a plate piled with sandwiches, another one full of cake, a large glass of Pimms - complete with floating fruit and ice cubes, and a large portion of strawberries and cream.

Andy grabbed the bowl of strawberries to shift it into the shade, only to spot a scrap of folded paper hiding underneath it. It started to dance across the tray, and he reached out and caught it just as it was about to blow away.

Unfolding it, Andy grinned as he stared at the large, loopy handwriting.

Save the biggest one for me. C x

CHAPTER 17

CATH

'Gather around, everyone!' yelled Cath. 'Gather around!'

Cath paused, but she didn't need to wait too long for the crowd to turn and face her. She was standing on a bit of makeshift staging Fergus had set up in front of the marquee. Beaming back at her were hundreds of Crumbleton residents. Some were wearing tennis whites, and all of them seemed to have a treat of some kind in their hands—whether it was one of the last few remaining portions of strawberries or an expertly mixed mocktail.

Every single face was smiling and happy—pink from a day of sunshine and laughter. Cath smiled back… a little nervously. Sure, she might have been dashing around all day, making sure everything was running smoothly, but she hadn't been at the centre of attention. Until now.

Cath took a deep breath, doing her best to steady her racing heart. She didn't really know why she was feeling so unsure all of a sudden... after all, the event had been a resounding success. The joyful faces in front of her were all the proof she needed. Still, there were things that needed to be said, news that needed to be shared... and a champion that needed to be celebrated.

Cath's eyes raked the crowd, searching for the one face she knew would give her the confidence she needed to address this crowd of strangers who already felt like they were well on their way to being friends.

There he was. Cath broke into a broad smile of her own as her eyes locked with Andy's. He was standing off to one side, his hands in his pockets and his lopsided grin making her want to run over to him and...

Cath cleared her throat.

'Thank you,' she said loudly and clearly, not taking her eyes off Andy for several long seconds. 'Thank you all for such a wonderful day,' she continued, tearing her eyes away from his, and letting them sweep over the rest of the crowd.

'Before we celebrate our new champion, I just wanted to say this...' she took a deep breath. 'After a very quick count of all the money raised today—I'm so excited to say that your museum is safe for the coming year.'

The roar of applause that greeted the news was

enough to bring tears to Cath's eyes. She blinked hard and cleared her throat, waiting for the noise to die down again.

'That's not all.' She continued. 'Not only has Fergus graciously hosted our event today, but he's also donated half the bar's takings to the Museum fund. He's just let me know the total so far... and this generous donation means that crucial repairs to the building will be able to start... straight away!'

The crowd started to roar again, and Cath grinned as she watched Fergus disappear under a good-natured scrum of hugs and back-pats.

'There's no way I'm going to be able to stand here and thank everyone who's made today possible—because we'd still be going at midnight,' said Cath, earning herself a wave of laughter.

She took a breath and hunted for Andy again, her eyes locking with his. 'Just know this... Crumbleton is amazing. I've not been here long, but you've all been behind me on this hair-brained plan from the start. Every single one of you here has made this event an absolute joy. Thank you for making it happen.'

'Three cheers for Cath!' boomed Geraldine from the front of the crowd.

Cath felt her cheeks flame hot and bright as the *Hip Hip Hoorays* made the staging underneath her feet vibrate.

'Thanks,' she laughed when the cheering calmed down a bit. 'Okay, we've got a champion to celebrate… and to award the cup, we have our very own celebrity.'

A murmur of excitement ran around the grass court.

'Please put your hands together for the 1988 Cheswell Cup champion… Evelyn Barker!'

Cath clapped and cheered along with the rest of the town as Evelyn made her way onto the platform, beaming from ear to ear and waving regally at everyone.

Geraldine stepped forward holding the huge, silver cup—which had been beautifully polished for the occasion. She passed it up to Cath, who then carefully handed it over to Evelyn before stepping down off the platform to make a bit of room.

'Ladies and gentlemen,' said Evelyn, her voice quavering with excitement. 'A round of applause for today's wonderful champion. I give you Kendra Lenglen – winner of the Sir Anthony Cheswell Cup, 2024!'

Cath watched as Kendra bounced onto the platform and accepted the cup from a beaming Evelyn, before taking the old lady's hand and raising it in the air.

'And the crowd went wild!' Andy's voice whispered in her ear, as everyone around them erupted into yet another round of cheering and applause.

'Can I kiss you now?' said Cath.

'Here?' said Andy, his eyebrows raised as she turned to face him.

'Here,' said Cath, resting her hands against his chest.

Andy broke into a smile and nodded, before wrapping his arms around her waist and drawing her towards him.

He tasted of strawberries.

'About bloomin' time!' Annie Pottinger's voice shouted from somewhere in the crowd as a round of clapping and giggling rippled around them in the late afternoon sunshine.

EPILOGUE

CRUMBLETON TIMES AND ECHO - 5TH SEPTEMBER

Love Match: Anonymous Donor Serves Up a Grand Slam Gift!

The excitement following the recent return of the Sir Anthony Cheswell Cup is far from over. Following this paper's social media coverage of the event in action, we were contacted by an anonymous donor wishing to ensure the future of Crumbleton Museum. The resulting six-figure donation will enable the development of the museum as a local historical and community hub over the next five years – under the watchful eye of our much-loved Cath Walker!

Curating Crumbleton – Museum's First Volunteer Meeting

Love our museum? Love to get involved? Join Cath at

the museum on Thursday afternoons from 1pm – 4pm and be prepared to roll your sleeves up. Telephone lead volunteer Evelyn Barker on local 876 to let her know you're coming, so that she can buy enough biscuits. Hard hats and safety gear provided.

Stop Throwing Things At Our Andy!

Andy Morgan would like to respectfully request that *everyone* stops throwing things at him while he works on the cobbles. He stated that—although the recent trend for tossing confetti at him is a lot less painful than cola cubes, it is quite embarrassing when there are tourists around who aren't in on the joke, and it gets stuck around the cobbles.

(Ed. Note: We're not just looking at the youngsters anymore, either! If you carry on, I'll start naming and shaming you in the paper... Annie! Oh look. I did it early.)

Caroline Cook. Editor

THE END

ALSO BY BETH RAIN

Seabury Series:

Welcome to Seabury (Seabury Book 1)

Trouble in Seabury (Seabury Book 2)

Christmas in Seabury (Seabury Book 3)

Sandwiches in Seabury (Seabury Book 4)

Secrets in Seabury (Seabury Book 5)

Surprises in Seabury (Seabury Book 6)

Dreams and Ice Creams in Seabury (Seabury Book 7)

Mistakes and Heartbreaks in Seabury (Seabury Book 8)

Laughter and Happy Ever After in Seabury (Seabury Book 9)

A Quiet Life in Seabury (Seabury Book 10)

In A Spin in Seabury (Seabury Book 11)

Living The Dream in Seabury (Seabury Book 12)

A Big Day in Seabury (Seabury Book 13)

Something Borrowed in Seabury (Seabury Book 14)

A Match Made in Seabury (Seabury Book 15)

Seabury Series Collections:

Kate's Story: Books 1 - 3

Hattie's Story: Books 4 - 6

Standalones: Books 7 - 9

Lizzie's Story: Books 10 - 12

Upper Bamton Series:

Upper Bamton: The Complete Series Collection: Books 1 - 4

Individual titles:

A New Arrival in Upper Bamton (Upper Bamton Book 1)

Rainy Days in Upper Bamton (Upper Bamton Book 2)

Hidden Treasures in Upper Bamton (Upper Bamton Book 3)

Time Flies By in Upper Bamton (Upper Bamton Book 4)

Standalone Books:

How to be Angry at Christmas

Crumbleton Series:

Coming Home to Crumbleton (Crumbleton Book 1)

Flowers Go Flying in Crumbleton (Crumbleton Book 2)

Match Point in Crumbleton (Crumbleton Book 3)

A Very Crumbleton Christmas (Crumbleton Book 4)

Little Bamton Series:

Little Bamton: The Complete Series Collection: Books 1 - 5

Individual titles:

Christmas Lights and Snowball Fights (Little Bamton Book 1)

Spring Flowers and April Showers (Little Bamton Book 2)

Summer Nights and Pillow Fights (Little Bamton Book 3)

Autumn Cuddles and Muddy Puddles (Little Bamton Book 4)

Christmas Flings and Wedding Rings (Little Bamton Book 5)

Crumcarey Island Series:

Crumcarey Island Series Collection: Books 1 - 5

Individual titles:

Christmas on Crumcarey (Crumcarey Island Book 1)

All Change on Crumcarey (Crumcarey Island Book 2)

Making Waves on Crumcarey (Crumcarey Island Book 3)

Fool's Gold on Crumcarey (Crumcarey Island Book 4)

A Fresh Start on Crumcarey (Crumcarey Island Book 5)

WRITING AS BEA FOX

What's a Girl To Do? The Complete Series

Individual titles:

The Holiday: What's a Girl To Do? (Book 1)

The Wedding: What's a Girl To Do? (Book 2)

The Lookalike: What's a Girl To Do? (Book 3)

The Reunion: What's a Girl To Do? (Book 4)

At Christmas: What's a Girl To Do? (Book 5)

ABOUT THE AUTHOR

Beth Rain has always wanted to be a writer and has been penning adventures for characters ever since she learned to stare into the middle-distance and daydream.

She recently moved to a windswept, Scottish island, and it is a dream come true to spend her days hanging out with Bob – her trusty laptop – scoffing crisps and chocolate while dreaming up swoony love stories for all her imaginary friends.

Beth's writing will always deliver on the happy-ever-afters, so if you need cosy… you're in safe hands!

Visit www.bethrain.com for all the bookish goodness and keep up with all Beth's news by joining her newsletter!

facebook.com/BethRainBooks
twitter.com/bethrainauthor
instagram.com/bethrainauthor

Printed in Great Britain
by Amazon